RUFUS AND ROSE

RAGGED DICK SERIES
BY
HORATIO ALGER JR.

RUFUS AND ROSE

RUFUS AND ROSE

OR

THE FORTUNES
OF ROUGH AND READY

BY

HORATIO ALGER, JR.

AUTHOR OF
"RAGGED DICK," "FAME AND FORTUNE,"
"MARK, THE MATCH BOY," "ROUGH AND READY,"
"BEN, THE LUGGAGE BOY," "CAMPAIGN SERIES,"
"LUCK AND PLUCK SERIES," ETC.

BottomoftheHillPublishing.com

ISBN: 978-1-4837-0518-7

To
MY YOUNG FRIENDS,
HENRY AND EUGENE,
THIS VOLUME
IS AFFECTIONATELY DEDICATED

Content

PREFACE

In presenting to the public the last volume of the "Ragged Dick Series," the author desires to return his thanks for the generous reception accorded, both by the press and the public, to these stories of street life. Several of the characters are drawn from life, and *nearly all* of the incidents are of actual occurrence. Indeed, the materials have been found so abundant that invention has played but a subordinate part.

The principal object proposed, in the preparation of these volumes, has been to show that the large class of street boys—numbering thousands in New York alone—furnishes material out of which good citizens may be made, if the right influences are brought to bear upon them. In every case, therefore, the author has led his hero, step by step, from vagabondage to a position of respectability; and, in so doing, has incurred the charge, in some quarters, of exaggeration. It can easily be shown, however, that he has fallen short of the truth, rather than exceeded it. In proof, the following extract from an article in a New York daily paper is submitted:—

"As a class, the newsboys of New York are worthy of more than common attention. The requirements of the trade naturally tend to develop activity both of mind and body, and, in looking over some historical facts, we find that *many of our most conspicuous public men* have commenced their careers as newsboys. Many of the principal offices of our city government and our chief police courts testify to the truth of this assertion. From the West we learn that many of the most enterprising journalists spring from the same stock."

Not long since, while on a western journey, the Superintendent of the Lodging House in Park Place found one of his boys filling the position of District Attorney in a western State, another settled as a clergyman, and still others prosperous and even wealthy business men. These facts are full of encouragement for those who are laboring to redeem and elevate the street boy, and train him up to fill a respectable position in society.

Though the six volumes already issued complete his original purpose, the author finds that he has by no means exhausted his subject, and is induced to announce a second series, devoted to still other phases of street life. This will shortly be commenced, under the general name of the "Tattered Tom Series."

New York, November 1, 1870.

CHAPTER I

NEW PLANS

"So this is to be your first day in Wall Street, Rufus," said Miss Manning.

"Yes," said Rufus, "I've retired from the newspaper business on a large fortune, and now I'm going into business in Wall Street just to occupy my time."

The last speaker was a stout, well-grown boy of fifteen, with a pleasant face, calculated to inspire confidence. He looked manly and self-reliant, and firm of purpose. For years he had been a newsboy, plying his trade in the streets of New York, and by his shrewdness, and a certain ready wit, joined with attention to business, he had met with better success than most of his class. He had been a leader among them, and had received the name of "Rough and Ready," suggested in part, no doubt, by his name, Rufus; but the appellation described not inaptly his prominent traits. He understood thoroughly how to take care of himself, and thought it no hardship, that, at an age when most boys are tenderly cared for, he was sent out into the streets to shift for himself.

His mother had been dead for some time. His step-father, James Martin, was a drunkard, and he had been compelled to take away his little sister Rose from the miserable home in which he had kept her, and had undertaken to support her, as well as himself. He had been fortunate enough to obtain a home for her with Miss Manning, a poor seamstress, whom he paid for her services in taking care of Rose. His step-father, in order to thwart and torment him, had stolen the little girl away, and kept her in Brooklyn for a while, until Rufus got a clue to her whereabouts, and succeeded in getting her back. At the time when the story opens, he had just recovered her, and having been fortunate enough to render an important service to Mr. Turner, a Wall Street broker, was on this Monday morning to enter his office, at a salary of eight dollars a week.

This sketch of the newsboy's earlier history is given for the benefit of those who have not read the book called "Rough and Ready," in which it is related at length. It is necessary to add that Rufus was in some sense a capitalist, having five hundred dollars deposited in a savings-bank to his credit. Of this sum, he had found three hundred one day, which, as no claimant ever appeared for it, he had been justified in appropriating to his own use. The remainder had been given him by Mr. Turner, in partial acknowledgment of the service before referred to.

"Your new life will seem strange to you at first, Rufus," said Miss Manning.

"Yes, it does already. When I woke up this morning, I was going to jump out of bed in a hurry, thinking I must go round to Nassau Street to get my papers. Then all at once I thought that I'd given up being a newsboy. But it seemed queer."

"I didn't know but you'd gone back to your old business," said the seamstress, pointing to a paper in his hand.

"It's this morning's 'Herald,'" explained Rufus; "you and Rose will have to be looking for another room where Martin can't find you. You'll find two columns of advertisements of 'Boarders and Lodgers Wanted,' so you can take your choice."

"I'll go out this morning," said the seamstress.

"All right. Take Rose along with you, or you may find her missing when you get back."

There was considerable reason to fear that the step-father, James Martin, would make a fresh attempt to get possession of Rose, and Rufus felt that it was prudent to guard against this.

"Have you had breakfast, Rufus?"

"Yes; I got breakfast at the Lodging House."

Here it may be remarked that Rufus had enjoyed advantages superior to most of his class, and spoke more correctly in general, but occasionally fell into modes of pronunciation such as he was accustomed to hear from his street associates. He had lately devoted a part of his evenings to study, under the superintendence of Miss Manning, who, coming originally from a country home, had had a good common-school education.

"It's time I was going down to the office," said Rufus. "Good-morning, Miss Manning. Good-morning, Rosy," as he stooped to kiss his little sister, a pretty little girl of eight.

"Good-morning, Rufie. Don't let Mr. Martin carry you off."

"I think he'd have a harder job to carry me off than you, Rosy," said Rufus, laughing. "Don't engage lodgings on Fifth Avenue, Miss Manning. I'm afraid it would take more than I can earn in Wall Street to pay my share of the expense."

"I shall be content with an humbler home," said the seamstress, smiling.

Rufus left the little room, which, by the way, looked out on Franklin Street near the Hudson River, and the seamstress, taking the "Herald," turned to the column of "Boarders and Lodgers Wanted."

There was a long list, but the greater part of the rooms advertised were quite beyond her slender means. Remembering that it would be prudent to get out of their present neighborhood, in order to put the drunken step-father off the track, she looked for places farther up town. The objection to this, however, was, that prices advance as you go up town. Still the streets near the river are not considered so eligible, and she thought that they might find something there. She therefore marked one place on Spring Street, another on Leroy Street, and still another, though with some hesitation, on Christopher Street. She feared that Rufus would object to this as too far up town.

"Now put on your things, Rose, and we'll take a walk."

"That will be nice," said Rose, and the little girl ran to get her shawl and bonnet. When she was dressed for the street, Rose would hardly have been taken for the sister of a newsboy. She had a pretty face, full of vivacity and intelligence, and her brother's pride in her had led him to dress her better than might have been expected from his small means. Many children of families in good circumstances were less neatly and tastefully dressed than Rose.

Taking the little girl by the hand, Miss Manning led the way down the narrow staircase. It was far from a handsome house in which they had thus far made their home. The wall-paper was torn from the walls in places, revealing patches of bare plastering; there was a faded and worn oil-cloth upon the stairs, while outside the rooms at intervals, along the entry, were buckets of dirty water and rubbish, which had been temporarily placed there by the occupants. As it was Monday, washing was going on in several of the rooms, and the vapor arising from hot suds found its way into the entry from one or two half-open doors. On the whole, it was not a nice or savory home, and the seamstress felt no regret in leaving it. But the question was, would she be likely to find a better.

The seamstress made her way first to Spring Street. She was led to infer, from the advertisement, that she might find cheap accommodations. But when she found herself in front of the house designated, she found it so dirty and neglected in appearance that she did not feel like entering. She was sure it would not suit her.

Next she went to Leroy Street. Here she found a neat-looking three-story brick house.

She rang the bell.

"You advertise a room to let," she said to the servant; "can I look at it?"

"I'll speak to the missis," said the girl.

Soon a portly lady made her appearance.

"You have a room to let?" said Miss Manning, interrogatively.

"Yes."

"Can I look at it?"

"It's for a gentleman," said the landlady. "I don't take ladies. Besides, it's rather expensive;" and she glanced superciliously at the plain attire of the seamstress.

Of course there was no more to be said. So Miss Manning and Rose found their way into the street once more.

The last on the list was Christopher Street.

"Come, Rose. Are you tired of walking?"

"Oh, no," said the child; "I can walk ever so far without getting tired."

Christopher Street is only three blocks from Leroy. In less than ten minutes they found themselves before the house advertised. It was a fair-looking house, but the seamstress found, on inquiry, that the room was a large one on the second floor, and that the rent would be beyond her means. She was now at the end of her list.

"I think, Rose," she said, "we will go to Washington Square, and sit down on one of the seats. I shall have to look over the paper again."

This square is a park of considerable size, comprising very nearly ten acres. Up to 1832, it had been for years used as a Potter's Field, or public cemetery, and it is estimated that more than one hundred thousand bodies were buried there. But in 1832 it became a park. There is a basin and a fountain in the centre, and it is covered with trees of considerable size. At frequent intervals there are benches for the accommodation of those who desire to pass an hour or two in the shade of the trees. In the afternoon, particularly, may be seen a large number of children playing in the walks, and nurse-maids drawing their young charges in carriages, or sitting with them on the seats.

Rose was soon busied in watching the sports of some children of her own age, while Miss Manning carefully scanned the advertisements. But she found nothing to reward her search. At length her attention was drawn to the following advertisement:—

"No. —, Waverley Place. Two small rooms. Terms reasonable."

"That must be close by," thought the seamstress.

She was right, for Waverley Place, commencing at Broadway, runs along the northern side of Washington Square. Before the up-town movement commenced, it was a fashionable quarter, and even now, as may be inferred from the character of the houses, is a very nice and respectable street, particularly that part which fronts the square.

Miss Manning could see the number mentioned from where she was seated, and saw at a glance that it was a nice house. Of course it was beyond her means,—she said that to herself; still, prompted by an impulse which she did not attempt to resist, she determined to call and make inquiries about the rooms advertised.

CHAPTER II

THE HOUSE IN WAVERLEY PLACE

Leaving the Park, Miss Manning crossed the street, went up the front steps of a handsome house, and rang the bell.

"What a nice house!" said Rose, admiringly; "are we going to live here?"

"No, I don't think we can afford it; but I will ask to see the rooms."

Soon the door was opened, and a servant-girl looked at them inquiringly.

"Can I see the rooms you have to let?" asked the seamstress.

"Step in a moment, and I'll call Mrs. Clayton."

They stepped into a hall, and remained waiting till a woman of middle age, with a pleasant countenance, came up from below, where she had been superintending the servants.

"I saw your advertisement of rooms to let," commenced Miss Manning, a little timidly, for she knew that the house was a finer one than with her limited means she could expect to enter, and felt a little like a humbug.

"Yes, I have two small rooms vacant."

"Are they—expensive?" asked the seamstress, with hesitation.

"I ought to say that only one is at my disposal," said the landlady; "and that is a hall bedroom on the third floor back. The other is a square room, nicely furnished, on the upper floor, large enough for two. But last evening, after I had sent in the advertisement, Mrs. Colman, who occupies my second floor front, told me she intended to get a young lady to look after her two little girls during the day, and teach them, and would wish her to occupy the larger room. I thought when I first saw you that you were going to apply for the situation."

A sudden thought came to Miss Manning. Why could she not undertake this office? It would pay her much better than sewing, and the children would be companions for Rose.

"How old are the little girls?" she said.

"One is five, the other seven, years old. Mrs. Colman is an invalid, and does not feel able to have the children with her all the time."

"Is Mrs. Colman at home?"

"Yes. Would you like to see her?"

"I should. I am fond of children, and I might be willing to undertake the charge of hers, if she thought fit to intrust them to me."

"I think it quite likely you can come to an agreement. She was wondering this morning where she could hear of a suitable person. Wait here a moment, and I will go and speak to her."

Mrs. Clayton went upstairs, and returned shortly.

"Mrs. Colman would like to see you," she said. "I will lead the way."

Miss Manning followed the landlady upstairs, and was ushered into a large, handsomely furnished room on the second floor. There was a cheerful fire in the grate, and beside it, in an easy-chair, sat a lady, looking nervous and in delicate health. Two little girls, who seemed full of the health and vitality which their mother lacked, were romping noisily on the floor.

"Mrs. Colman," said the landlady, "this is the young lady I spoke of."

"Take a seat, please," said Mrs. Colman, politely. "I am an invalid as you see, Mrs. ——?" here she looked up inquiringly.

"Miss Manning," said the seamstress.

"Then the little girl is not yours?"

"Not mine; but I have the care of her, as her mother is dead."

"How old is she?"

"Eight."

"A little older than my Jennie. Are you fond of children, Miss Manning?"

"Very much so."

"I am looking for some one who will look after my little girls during the day, and teach them. At present they know absolutely nothing, and I have not been willing to send them out of the house to school. What I have been thinking is, of securing some one who would live in the house, and take the care of the children off my hands. I am an invalid, as you see, and sometimes their noise absolutely distracts me."

Miss Manning was struck with pity, as she noticed the pale, nervous face of the invalid.

"Then the children need to go out and take a walk every day; but I have no one to send with them. You wouldn't object to that, would you?"

"No, I should like it."

"Could you come soon?"

"I could come to-morrow, if you desire it," said Miss Manning, promptly.

"I wish you would. I have a nervous headache which will last me some days, I suppose, and the children can't keep still. I suppose it is their nature to be noisy."

"I can take them out for an hour now, if you like it, Mrs. Colman. It would give me a chance to get acquainted."

"Would you? It would be quite a relief to me, and to them too. Oh, there is one thing we must speak of. What compensation will satisfy you?"

"I don't know how much I ought to ask. I am willing to leave that matter to you."

"You would want your little girl to live with you, I suppose."

"Yes, she needs me to look after her."

"Very well. Then I will pay Mrs. Clayton for the board of both of you, and if two dollars a week would satisfy you—"

Would satisfy her? Miss Manning's breath was quite taken away at the magnificent prospect that opened before her. She could hardly conceive it possible that her services were worth a home in so nice a house and two dollars a week besides. Why, toiling early and late at her needle, she had barely earned hitherto, thirty-seven cents a day, and out of that all her expenses had to be paid. Now she would still be able to sew while the children were learning their lessons. She would no longer be the occupant of a miserable tenement house, but would live in a nice quarter of the city. She felt devoutly thankful for the change: but, on the whole, considered that perhaps it was not best to let Mrs. Colman see just how glad she was. So she simply expressed herself as entirely satisfied with the terms that were offered. Mrs. Colman seemed glad that this matter had been so easily arranged.

"Mrs. Clayton will show you the room you are to occupy," she said. "I have not been into it, but I understand that it is very comfortable. If there is any addition in the way of furniture which you may require, I will make it at my own expense."

"Thank you. You are very kind."

Here Mrs. Clayton reappeared, and, at the request of Mrs. Colman, offered to show them the room which they were to occupy.

"It is on the upper floor," she said, apologetically; "but it is of good size and pleasant, when you get to it."

She led the way into the room. It was, as she had said, a pleasant one, well lighted, and of good size. A thick woollen carpet covered the floor; there were a bureau, a clothes-press, a table, and other articles needful to make it comfortable. After the poor room they had occupied, it looked very attractive.

"I think I shall like it," said Miss Manning, with satisfaction.

"Are we to live here?" asked Rose, who had not quite understood the nature of the arrangement.

"Yes, Rosy; do you think you shall like it?"

"Oh, yes, ever so much. When are we coming?"

"To-morrow morning. You will have two little girls to play with."

"The little girls I saw in that lady's room downstairs?"

"Yes. Do you think you shall like it?"

"I think it will be very nice," said Rose, with satisfaction.

"Well, how do you like the room, Miss Manning?" said Mrs. Colman, when they had returned from upstairs.

"It looks very pleasant. I have no doubt I shall like it."

"I think you will need a rocking-chair and a sofa. I will ask Mr. Colman to step into some upholsterer's as he goes down town to-morrow, and send them up. If it wouldn't be too much trouble, Miss Manning, I will ask you to help Carrie and Jennie on with their hats and cloaks. They quite enjoy the thought of a run out of doors with you and your little girl. By the way, what is her name?"

"Rose."

"A very pretty name. I have no doubt the three children will soon become excellent friends. She seems a nice little girl."

"Rose is a nice little girl," said the seamstress, affectionately.

In a short time they were on their way downstairs. In the hall below they met the landlady once more.

"What is the price of your hall bedroom, Mrs. Clayton?" asked Miss Manning.

"Five dollars and a half a week," was the answer.

It needs to be mentioned that this was in the day of low prices, and that such an apartment now, with board, would cost at least twelve dollars a week.

"What made you ask, Miss Manning?" said Rose.

"I was thinking that perhaps Rufus might like to take it."

"Oh, I wish he would," said Rose; "then we would all be together."

"We are speaking of her brother," said Miss Manning, turning to Mrs. Clayton.

"How old is he?"

"Fifteen."

"Is he at school, or in a place?"

"He is in a broker's office in Wall Street."

"Then, as he is the little girl's brother, I will say only five dollars a week for the room."

"Thank you, Mrs. Clayton. I will let you know what he decides upon to-morrow."

They went out to walk, going as far as Union Square, where Miss Manning sat down on a bench, and let the children sport at will. It is needless to say that they very soon got well acquainted, and after an hour and a half, which their bright eyes testified to their having enjoyed, Miss Manning carried the little Colmans back to Waverley Place, and, with Rose, took the horse-cars back to their old home.

"Won't Rufie be surprised when he hears about it?" said Rose.

"Yes, Rosy, I think he will," said Miss Manning.

CHAPTER III

JAMES MARTIN'S VICISSITUDES

While Miss Manning is seeking a new boarding-place for herself and Rose, events are taking place in Brooklyn which claim our attention. It is here that James Martin, the shiftless and drunken step-father of Rufus and Rose, has made a temporary residence. He had engaged board at the house of a widow, Mrs. Waters, and for two or three weeks paid his board regularly, being employed at his trade of a carpenter on some houses going up near by. But it was not in James Martin's nature to work steadily at anything. His love of drink had spoiled a once good and industrious workman, and there seemed to be little chance of any permanent improvement in his character or habits. For a time Rufus used to pay him over daily the most of his earnings as a newsboy, and with this he managed to live miserably enough without doing much himself. But after a while Rufus became tired of this arrangement, and withdrew himself and his sister to another part of the town, thus throwing Martin on his own resources. Out of spite Martin contrived to kidnap Rose, but, as we have seen, her brother had now succeeded in recovering her.

After losing Rose, Martin took the way back to his boarding-house, feeling rather doubtful of his reception from Mrs. Waters, to whom he was owing a week's board, which he was quite unable to pay. He had told her that he would pay the bill as soon as he could exchange a fifty-dollar note, which it is needless to say was only an attempt at deception, since he did not even possess fifty cents.

On entering the house, he went at once to his room, and lay down on the bed till the supper-bell rang. Then he came down, and took his place at the table with the rest of the boarders.

"Where's your little girl, Mr. Martin?" inquired Mrs. Waters, missing Rose.

"She's gone on a visit to some of her relations in New York," answered Martin, with some degree of truth.

"How long is she to stay?"

"Till she can have some new clothes made up; maybe two or

three weeks."

"That's rather sudden, isn't it? You didn't think of her going this morning?"

"No," answered Martin, with his mouth full of toast; "but she teased so hard to go, I let her. She's a troublesome child. I shall be glad to have the care of her off my mind for a time."

This might be true; but Mrs. Waters was beginning to lose confidence in Mr. Martin's statements. She felt that it was the part of prudence to make sure of the money he was already owing her, and then on some pretext get rid of him.

When supper was over, Martin rose, and was about to go out, but Mrs. Waters was too quick for him.

"Mr. Martin," she said, "may I speak to you a moment?"

"Yes, ma'am," answered Martin, turning reluctantly.

"I suppose you are ready to pay my bill; I need the money particularly."

"I'll pay it to-morrow, Mrs. Waters."

"You promised to pay me as soon as you changed a bill, and this morning you said you should have a chance to change it, as you were going to buy your little girl some new clothes."

"I know I did," said Martin, feeling cornered.

"I suppose, therefore, you can pay me the money to-night," said Mrs. Waters, sharply.

"Why, the fact is, Mrs. Waters," said Martin, awkwardly, "I was very unfortunate. As I was sitting in the horse-car coming home, I had my pocket picked of all the money I got in change. There was some over forty dollars."

"I'm sorry," said Mrs. Waters, coldly, for she did not believe a word of this; "but I need my money."

"If it hadn't been for that, I'd have paid you to-night."

"There's only one word I have to say, Mr. Martin," said the landlady, provoked; "if you can't pay me, you must find another boarding-place."

"I'll attend to it in a day or two. I guess I can get the money to-morrow."

"If you can't pay me to-night, you'll oblige me by giving up your room to-morrow morning. I'm a poor widder, Mr. Martin, and I must look out for number one. I can't afford to keep boarders that don't pay their bills."

There was one portion of this speech that set Mr. Martin to thinking. Mrs. Waters was a widow—he was a widower. By marrying her he would secure a home, and the money received from the boarders would be paid to him. He might not be accepted. Still it would do no harm to try.

"Mrs. Waters," he said, abruptly, wreathing his features into what he considered an attractive smile, "since I lost my wife I've been feeling very lonely. I need a wife to look after me and my little gal. If you will marry me, we'll live happy, and—"

"Thank you, Mr. Martin," said Mrs. Waters, considerably astonished at the sudden turn affairs had taken; "but I've got too much to do to think about marrying. Leastways, I don't care about marrying a man that can't pay his board-bill."

"Just as you say," answered Martin, philosophically; "I've give you a good chance. Perhaps you won't get another very soon."

"Well, if there isn't impudence for you!" ejaculated Mrs. Waters, as her boarder left the room. "I must be hard up for a husband, to marry such a shiftless fellow as he is."

The next morning, Mr. Martin made his appearance, as usual, at the breakfast-table. Notwithstanding his proposal of marriage had been so decidedly rejected the day before, his appetite was not only as good as usual, but considerably better. In fact, as he was not quite clear where his dinner was to come from, or whether, indeed, he should have any at all, he thought it best to lay in sufficient to last him for several hours. Mrs. Waters contemplated with dismay the rapid manner in which he disposed of the beef-steak and hash which constituted the principal dishes of her morning meal, and decided that the sooner she got rid of such a boarder the better.

Mr. Martin observed the eyes of the landlady fixed upon him, and misinterpreted it. He thought it possible she might have changed her mind as to the refusal of the day before, and resolved to renew his proposal. Accordingly he lingered till the rest of the boarders had left the table.

"Mrs. Waters," he said, "maybe you've changed your mind since yesterday."

"About what?" demanded the landlady, sharply.

"About marrying me."

"No, I haven't," answered the widow; "you needn't mention the matter again. When I want to marry you, I'll send and let you know."

"All right!" said Martin; "there's several after me, but I'll wait a week for you."

"Oh, don't trouble yourself," said the landlady, sarcastically; "I don't want to disappoint anybody else. Can you pay me this morning?"

"I'll have the money in a day or two."

"You needn't come back to dinner unless you bring the money to pay your bill. I can't afford to give you your board."

Mr. Martin rose and left the house, understanding pretty clearly that he couldn't return. On reaching the street, he opened his pocket-book, and ascertained that twelve cents were all it contained. This small amount was not likely to last very long. He decided to go to New York, having no further inducements to keep him in Brooklyn. Something might turn up, he reasoned, in the shiftless manner characteristic of him.

Jumping upon a passing car, he rode down to Fulton Ferry, and crossed in the boat to the New York side, thus expending for travelling expenses eight cents.

Supposing that Rufus still sold papers in front of the "Tribune" office, he proceeded to Printing House Square, and looked around for him; but he was nowhere to be seen.

"Who you lookin' for, gov'nor?" inquired a boot-black, rather short of stature, but with an old-looking face.

"Aint you the boy that went home with me Wednesday?" asked Martin, to whom Ben Gibson's face looked familiar.

"S'posin' I am?"

"Have you seen a newsboy they call Rough and Ready, this morning?"

"Don't you try to fool me."

"Yes, I seed him."

"Where is he? Has he sold all his papers?"

"He's giv' up sellin' papers, and gone into business on Wall Street."

"Don't you try to fool me, or I'll give you a lickin'," said Martin, sternly.

"Thank you for your kind offer," said Ben, "but lickings don't agree with my constitution."

"Why don't you tell me the truth then?"

"I did."

"You said Rufus had gone into business in Wall Street."

"So he has. A rich cove's taken a fancy to him, and adopted him as a office-boy."

"How much does he pay him?" asked Martin, considering whether there would be any chance of getting some money out of his step-son.

"Not knowin' can't say," replied Ben; "but he's just bought two pocket-books to hold his wages in."

"You're a humbug!" said Martin, indignantly. "What's the man's name he works for?"

"It's painted in big letters on the sign. You can't miss it."

James Martin considered, for an instant, whether it would be best to give Ben a thrashing, but the approach of a policeman led him to decide in the negative.

"Shine yer boots, gov'nor?" asked Ben, professionally.

"Yes," said Martin, rather unexpectedly.

"Payment in advance!" said Ben, who didn't think it prudent to trust in this particular instance.

"I'll tell yer what," said Martin, to whom necessity had taught a certain degree of cunning, "if you'll lend me fifty cents for a week, I'll let you shine my boots every day, and pay you the money besides."

"That's a very kind proposal," said Ben; "but I've just invested all my money on a country-seat up the river, which makes me rather short."

"Then you can't lend me the fifty?"

"No, but I'll tell you where you can get it."

"Where?"

"Up in Chatham Street. There's plenty'll lend it on the security of that hat of yours."

The hat in question was in the last stages of dilapidation, looking as if it had been run over daily by an omnibus, and then used to fill the place of a broken pane, being crushed out of all shape and comeliness.

Martin aimed a blow at Ben, but the boot-black dexterously evaded it, and, slinging his box over his back, darted down Nassau Street.

Later in the day he met Rough and Ready.

"I see the gov'nor this mornin'," said Ben.

"What, Mr. Martin?"

"Yes."

"What did he say?"

"He inquired after you in the most affectionate manner, and wanted to know where you was at work."

"I hope you didn't tell him."

"Not if I know myself. I told him he'd see the name on the sign. Then he wanted to borrow fifty cents for a week."

Rufus laughed.

"It's a good investment, Ben. I've invested considerable money that way. I suppose you gave him the money?"

"Maybe I did. He offered me the chance of blacking his boots every day for a week, if I'd lend him the money; but I had to resign the glorious privilege, not havin' been to the bank this mornin' to withdraw my deposits."

"You talk like a banker, Ben."

"I'm goin' to bankin' some day, when boot-blacking gets dull."

Ben Gibson had been for years a boot-black, having commenced the business when only eight years old. His life had been one of hardship and privation, as street life always is, but he had become toughened to it, and bore it with a certain stoicism, never complaining, but often joking in a rude way at what would have depressed and discouraged a more sensitive temperament. He was by no means a model boy, though not as bad as many of his class. He had learned to smoke and to swear, and did both freely. But there was a certain rude honesty about him which led Rufus, though in every way his superior, to regard him with friendly interest, and he had, on more than one occasion, been of considerable service to our hero in his newsboy days. Rufus had tried to induce him to give up smoking, but thus far without success.

"It keeps a feller warm," he said; "besides it won't hurt me. I'm tough."

CHAPTER IV

HOW JAMES MARTIN CAME TO GRIEF

After parting with Ben Gibson, James Martin crossed the street to the City Hall Park, and sat down on one of the wooden benches placed there for the public accommodation. Neither his present circumstances nor his future prospects were very brilliant. He was trying to solve the great problem which has troubled so many lazy people, of how best to live without work. There are plenty of men, not only in our cities, but in country villages, who are at work upon this same problem, but few solve it to their satisfaction. Martin was a good carpenter, and might have earned a respectable and comfortable livelihood, instead of wandering about the streets in ragged attire, without a roof to shelter him, or money to pay for a decent meal.

As he sat on the bench, a cigar-boy passed him, with a box of cigars under his arm.

"Cigars," he cried, "four for ten cents!"

"Come here, boy," said Martin. The boy approached.

"I want a cigar."

"I don't sell one. Four for ten cents."

Martin would willingly have bought four, but as his available funds amounted only to four cents, this was impossible.

"I don't want but one; I've only got four cents in change, unless you can change a ten-dollar bill."

"I can't do that."

"Here, take three cents, and give me a prime cigar."

"I'll sell you one for four cents."

"Hand over, then."

So Martin found himself penniless, but the possessor of a cigar, which he proceeded to smoke with as much apparent enjoyment as if he had a large balance to his credit at the bank.

He remained in the Park till his cigar was entirely smoked, and then sauntered out with no definite object in view. It occurred to him, however, that he might as well call on the keeper of a liquor saloon on Baxter Street, which he had frequently patronized.

"How are you, Martin?" asked "Jim," that being the name by

which the proprietor was generally known.

"Dry as a fish," was the suggestive reply.

"Then you've come to the right shop. What'll you have?"

Martin expressed his desire for a glass of whiskey, which was poured out, and hastily gulped down.

"I'm out of stamps," said Martin, coolly. "I s'pose you'll trust me till to-morrow."

"Why didn't you say you hadn't any money?" demanded Jim, angrily.

"Come," said Martin, "don't be hard on an old friend. I'll pay you to-morrow."

"Where'll the money come from?" demanded Jim, suspiciously.

This was a question which Martin was quite unable to answer satisfactorily to himself.

"I'll get it some way," he answered.

"You'd better, or else you needn't come into this shop again."

Martin left the saloon rather disappointed. He had had a little idea of asking a small loan from his friend "Jim;" but he judged that such an application would hardly be successful under present circumstances. "Jim's" friendship evidently was not strong enough to justify such a draft upon it.

Martin began to think that it might have been as well, on the whole, to seek employment at his trade in Brooklyn, for a time at least, until he could have accumulated a few dollars. It was rather uncomfortable being entirely without money, and that was precisely his present condition. Even if he had wanted to go back to Brooklyn, he had not even the two cents needed to pay the boat fare. Matters had come to a crisis with Martin financially, and a suspension of specie payments was forced upon him.

He continued to walk about the streets in that aimless way which results from absence of occupation, and found it, on the whole, rather cheerless work. Besides, he was beginning to get hungry. He had eaten a hearty breakfast at his boarding-house in Brooklyn, but it was now one o'clock, and the stomach began to assert its claims once more. He had no money. Still there were places where food, at least, could be had for nothing. He descended into a subterranean apartment, over the door of which was a sign bearing the words Free Lunch.

As many of my readers know, these establishments are to be found in most of our cities. A supply of sandwiches, or similar food, is provided free for the use of those who enter, but visitors are expected to call and pay for one or more glasses of liquor, which are sold at such prices that the proprietor may, on the whole, realize a profit.

It was into one of those places that James Martin entered. He went up to the counter, and was about to help himself to the food supplied. After partaking of this, he intended to slip out without the drink, having no money to pay for it. But, unfortunately for the success of his plans, the keeper at the saloon had been taken in two or three times already that day by similar impostors. Still, had James Martin been well-dressed, he could have helped himself unquestioned to the provisions he desired. But his appearance was suspicious. His ragged and dirty attire betokened extreme poverty, and the man in charge saw, at a glance, that his patronage was not likely to be desirable.

"Look here, my friend," he said, abruptly, as Martin was about to help himself, "what'll you take to drink?"

"A glass of ale," said Martin, hesitatingly.

"All right! Pass over the money."

"The fact is," said Martin, "I left my pocket-book at home this morning, and that's why I'm obliged to come in here."

"Very good! Then you needn't trouble yourself to take anything. We don't care about visitors that leave their pocket-books at home."

"I'll pay you double to-morrow," said Martin, who had no hesitation in making promises he hadn't the least intention of fulfilling.

"That won't go down," said the other. "I don't care about seeing such fellows as you at any time. There's the door."

"Do you want to fight?" demanded Martin, angrily.

"No, I don't; but I may kick you out if you don't go peaceably. We don't want customers of your sort."

"I'll smash your head!" said Martin, becoming pugnacious.

"Here, Mike, run up and see if you can't find a policeman."

This hint was not lost upon Martin. He had no great love for the Metropolitan police, and kept out of their way as much as possible. He felt that it would be prudent to evacuate the premises, and did so, muttering threats meanwhile, and not without a lingering glance at the lunch which was not free to him.

This last failure rather disgusted Martin. According to his theory, the world owed him a living; but it seemed as if the world were disposed to repudiate the debt. Fasting is apt to lead to serious reflection, and by this time he was decidedly hungry. How to provide himself with a dinner was a subject that required immediate attention.

He walked about for an hour or two without finding himself at the end of that time any nearer the solution of the question than before. To work all day may be hard; but to do nothing all day on an empty stomach is still harder.

About four o'clock, Martin found himself at the junction of Wall Street and Nassau. I hardly know what drew this penniless man to the street through which flows daily a mighty tide of wealth, but I suspect that he was hoping to meet Rufus, who, as he had learned from Ben Gibson, was employed somewhere on the street. Rufus might, in spite of the manner in which he had treated him, prove a truer friend in need than the worthless companions of his hours of dissipation.

All at once a sharp cry of pain was heard.

A passing vehicle had run over the leg of a boy who had imprudently tried to cross the street just in front of it. The wheels passed over the poor boy's legs, both of which appeared to be broken. Of course, as is always the case under such circumstances, there was a rush to the spot where the casualty took place, and a throng of men and boys gathered about the persons who were lifting the boy from the ground.

"The boy seems to be poor," said a humane by-stander; "let us raise a little fund for his benefit."

A humane suggestion like this is pretty sure to be acted upon by those whose hearts are made tender by the sight of suffering. So most of those present drew out their pocket-books, and quite a little sum was placed in the hands of the original proposer of the contribution.

Among those who had wedged themselves into the crowd was James Martin. Having nothing to do, he had been eager to have his share in the excitement. He saw the collection taken up with an envious wish that it was for his own benefit. Beside him was a banker, who, from a plethoric pocket-book, had drawn a five-dollar bill, which he had contributed to the fund. Closing the pocket-book, he carelessly placed it in an outside pocket. James Martin stood in such a position that the contents of the pocket-book were revealed to him, and the demon of cupidity entered his heart. How much good this money would do him! There were probably several hundred dollars in all, perhaps more. He saw the banker put the money in his pocket,—the one nearest to him. He might easily take it without observation,—so he thought.

In an evil moment he obeyed the impulse which had come to him. He plunged his hand into the pocket; but at this moment the banker turned, and detected him.

"I've caught you, you rascal!" he exclaimed, seizing Martin with a vigorous grip. "Police!"

Martin made a desperate effort to get free, but another man seized him on the other side, and he was held, despite his resistance, till a policeman, who by a singular chance happened to be near when wanted, came up.

Martin's ragged coat was rent asunder from the violence of his efforts, his hat fell off, and he might well have been taken for a desperate character, as in this condition he was marched off by the guardian of the city's peace.

There was another humiliation in store for him. He had gone but a few steps when he met Rufus, who gazed in astonishment at his step-father's plight. Martin naturally supposed that Rufus would exult in his humiliation; but he did him injustice.

"I'm sorry for him," thought our hero, compassionately; "he's done me harm enough, but I'm sorry."

He learned from one of the crowd for what Martin had been arrested, and started for Franklin Street to carry the news to Miss Manning and Rose.

CHAPTER V

THE LAST EVENING IN FRANKLIN STREET

Though Rufus felt sorry for Mr. Martin's misfortune, there was at least one satisfaction connected with it. He would doubtless be sent to Blackwell's Island for three months, and of course when there he would be unable to annoy Rose, or contrive any plots for carrying her off. This would be a great relief to Rufus, who felt more than ever how much the presence of his little sister contributed to his happiness. If he was better than the average of the boys employed like himself, it was in a considerable measure due to the fact that he had never been adrift in the streets, but even in the miserable home afforded by his step-father had been unconsciously influenced towards good by the presence of his mother, and latterly by his little sister Rose. He, in his turn, had gained a salutary influence among the street boys, who looked up to him as a leader, though that leadership was gained in the first place by his physical superiority and manly bearing.

It occurred to him, that perhaps, after all, it might not be necessary for Rose and Miss Manning to move from Franklin Street at present, on account of Mr. Martin's arrest. He was rather surprised, when, on entering the little room, after hurrying upstairs two or three steps at a time, he saw Miss Manning's trunk open and half packed, with various articles belonging to herself and Rose spread out beside it.

"Hallo!" he exclaimed, stopping short on the threshold, "what are you doing?"

"Getting ready to move, Rufus," answered the seamstress.

"So you've found a place?"

"Oh, such a nice place, Rufie!" chimed in little Rose; "there's a nice carpet, and there's going to be a sofa, and oh, it's beautiful!"

"So you're going to live in style, are you?" said Rufus. "But how about the cost, Miss Manning?"

"That's the pleasantest part of it," was the reply; "it isn't going to cost me anything, and I am to be paid two dollars a week besides."

Rufus looked bewildered.

"Can't I get a chance there too?" he asked. "I'd be willin' to give 'em the pleasure of my society for half a price, say a dollar a week, besides a room."

"We are to be boarded also," said Miss Manning, in a tone of satisfaction.

"If it's a conundrum I'll give it up," said Rufus; "just tell a feller all about it, for I begin to think you're crazy, or else have come across some benevolent chap that's rather loose in the upper story."

Hereupon Miss Manning, unwilling to keep Rufus longer in suspense, gave him a full account of her morning's adventures, including her engagement with Mrs. Colman.

"You're in luck," said Rufus, "and I'm glad of it; but there's one thing we'll have to settle about."

"What's that?"

"About Rose's board."

"Oh, that is all settled already. Mrs. Colman is to pay for her board as well as mine."

"Yes, I know that; but it is your teachin' that is to pay for it."

"Yes, I suppose so."

"Then I must pay you for her board. That will make it all right."

"Oh, no, Rufus, I couldn't accept anything. You see it doesn't cost me anything."

"Yes, it does," persisted the newsboy; "if it wasn't for that, you would be paid more money."

"If it wasn't for her, I should not have applied for board in that place; so you see that it is to Rose, after all, that I am indebted for the situation."

"I see that you are very kind to Rose, Miss Manning, but I can't have you pay for her board. I am her brother, and am well and strong. I can afford to pay for Rose, and I will. Now how much will it be?"

Miss Manning persisted that she was not willing to receive anything; but upon this point the newsboy's pride was aroused, and finally this arrangement was made: Miss Manning was to receive three dollars a week, and for this sum she also agreed to provide Rose with proper clothing, so that Rufus would have no responsibility or care about her. He wanted the seamstress to accept four dollars; but upon this point she was quite determined. She declared that three dollars was too high, but finally agreed to accept it.

"I don't want to make money out of Rose," she said.

"It'll take some time to get ahead of A. T. Stewart on three dollars a week."

"I shall have five dollars a week."

"But you will have to buy clothes for Rose and yourself."

"I shall make them myself, so that they won't cost me more than half of the money."

"Then you can save up the rest."

"But you will only have five dollars left to pay your expenses, Rufus."

"Oh, I can get along. Don't mind me."

"But I wanted you to come and board with us. Mrs. Clayton has a hall bedroom which she would let to you with board for five dollars a week. But that would leave you nothing for clothes."

"I could earn enough some other way to pay for my clothes," said Rufus; "but I don't know about going to board with you. I expect it's a fashionable place, and I shouldn't know how to behave."

"You will know how to behave as well as I do. I didn't think you were bashful, Rufus."

"No more I am in the street," said the newsboy; "but you know how I've lived, Miss Manning. Mr. Martin didn't live in fashionable style, and his friends were not very select. When I took breakfast at Mr. Turner's, I felt like a cat in a strange garret."

"Then it's time you got used to better society," said Miss Manning. "You want to rise in the world, don't you?"

"Of course I do."

"Then take my advice, and come with us. You'll soon get used to it."

"Maybe I will. I'll come round to-morrow, and see how I like it."

"Remember you are in business in Wall Street, and ought to live accordingly. Don't you think Mr. Turner would prefer to have you board in a good place rather than sleep at the Lodging House, without any home of your own?"

"Yes, I suppose he would," said Rufus.

The idea was a new one to him, but it was by no means disagreeable. He had always been ambitious to rise, but thus far circumstances had prevented his gratifying this ambition. His stepfather's drunken habits, and the consequent necessity he was under of contributing to his support as well as that of Rose, and his mother when living, had discouraged him in all his efforts, and led him to feel that all his efforts were unavailing. But now his fortunes had materially changed. Now, for the first time, there seemed to be a chance for him. He felt that it was best to break off, as far as possible, his old life, and turn over a new leaf. So the advice of his friend, Miss Manning, commended itself to his judgment, and he about made up his mind to become a boarder at Mrs. Clayton's. He would have the satisfaction of being in the same house with his little sister Rose, and thus of seeing much more of her than if he boarded down town at the Lodging House. It would cost him more to be sure, leaving him, as Miss Manning suggested, nothing for his clothes; but, as his duties in Wall Street did not commence until nine o'clock, and terminated at five, he felt sure that in his leisure time he would be able to earn enough to meet this expense. Besides, there would be the interest on his five hundred dollars, which would amount to not less than thirty dollars, and probably more, for, with the advice of Mr. Turner, he was about to purchase with it some bank shares. Then, if it should be absolutely necessary, he could break in upon his principal, although he would be sorry to do this, for, though he did not expect to add to it for a year to come, he hoped to keep it at its present amount.

These thoughts passed rapidly through his mind, and, when little Rose, taking his hand, said, pleadingly, "Do come and live with us, Rufie!" he answered, "Yes, Rosy, I will, if Mrs. Clayton will make room for me."

"Oh, that will be so nice, won't it, Miss Manning?" said Rose, clapping her hands.

"Perhaps Mr. Martin will come and board with us," said Rufus, jestingly; "wouldn't you like that, Rose?"

"No," said Rose, looking frightened; "do you think he will find out where we are?"

"Not for some time at least," said her brother. "By the way, I saw him to-day, Miss Manning."

"Did you speak with him, Rufus?"

"Did he try to carry you off, Rufie?" asked Rose, anxiously.

"You forget, Rose, that I am rather too big to carry off," said Rufus. "No, he did not say anything to me. The fact is, he has got into a scrape, and has enough to do to think of himself."

"Tell us about it, Rufus."

"I saw him, just as I was coming home, in the hands of the police. I heard that he had tried to rob a gentleman of his pocket-book."

"What will they do to him?"

"I suppose he will be sent to the Island."

"I am sorry for him, though he has not treated you and Rose right."

"Yes, I am sorry too; but at any rate we need not feel anxious about his getting hold of Rose."

They had a very pleasant supper together. It was the last supper in the old room, and they determined that it should be a good one. Rufus went out and got some sirloin steak, and brought in a pie from the baker's. This, with what they had already had, made a very nice supper.

"You won't have any more cooking to do for some time, Miss Manning," said Rufus; "you'll be a lady, with servants to wait on you. I hope the two little girls won't give you much trouble. If they do, that might be harder work than sewing."

"They seem to be quite pleasant little girls, and they will be a good deal of company for Rose."

"How did you like them, Rosie?" asked her brother.

"Ever so much. Jennie,—that's the oldest, you know, she's almost as big as me,—said she would give me one of her dolls. She's got four."

"That's quite a large family for a young lady to have. Don't you think she would give me one of them?"

"Boys don't have dolls," said Rose, decidedly. "It aint proper."

Rufus laughed.

"Then I suppose I must do without one; but it would be a great deal of company for me when I go down town to business. I could put it in my pocket, you know."

"You're only making fun, Rufie."

"I suppose you think of going up to Mrs. Clayton's the first thing in the morning," said Rufus, turning to Miss Manning.

"Yes," she answered; "I can send up my trunk by a city express, and Rose and I can go up by the horse-cars, or, if it is pleasant, we will walk."

"I will go up with you, and look at the room you spoke of, if you will go early enough for me to be down at the office at nine o'clock."

Miss Manning assented to this arrangement, and Rufus left Franklin Street at nine, and repaired to the Newsboy's Lodging House, to sleep there for the last time.

CHAPTER VI

A NEW HOME

At an early hour the next morning Miss Manning, accompanied by Rufus and Rose, ascended Mrs. Clayton's steps, and rang the bell.

The summons was answered directly by a servant.

"Is Mrs. Clayton at home?" inquired Miss Manning.

"Yes; you're Mrs. Colman's new governess, aint you?"

"I am; but I would like to see Mrs. Clayton first."

"Come in, and I'll call her."

The three remained standing in the hall, awaiting the appearance of the landlady.

Rufus surveyed the interior of the house, so far as he could see it, with evident approval. Not that the house compared with the homes of many of my young readers who are favored by fortune. It was not magnificent, but it was neat, and well furnished, and looked bright and cheerful. To Rufus it appeared even elegant. He had a glimpse of the parlor through the half-opened door, and it certainly was so, compared with the humble boarding-house in Franklin Street, not to mention the miserable old tenement house on Leonard Street, which the readers of "Rough and Ready" will easily remember.

"I say, Miss Manning, this is jolly," said Rufus, in a tone of satisfaction.

"Isn't it a nice house, Rufie?" said little Rose.

"Yes, it is, Rosie;" and Rough and Ready, to call him for once by his old name, felt happy in the thought that his little sister, whose life, thus far, had been passed in a miserable quarter of the city, would now be so much more favorably situated.

At this moment Mrs. Clayton made her appearance.

"Good-morning, Miss Manning," she said, cordially; "I am sorry the servant left you standing in the hall. Good-morning, my dear," addressing Rose; "is this young man your brother?"

"He is my brother," said Rose; "but he isn't a young man. He's a boy."

Rufus smiled.

"Maybe I'll be a young man in twenty or thirty years," he said. "Miss Manning tells me," he continued, "that you have a small room which you will let for five dollars a week with board."

"Yes," said the landlady; "my price has always been five and a half, but as your sister would like to have you here, I will say five to you."

"Can I look at it?"

"Yes, I will go up and show it to you at once."

They followed Mrs. Clayton up two flights of stairs. The door of the vacant room was already open. It was a hall bedroom of ordinary size. The head of the bed was on the same side as the door, the room being just wide enough for it. Between the foot of the bed and the window, but on the opposite side, was a bureau with a mirror. There were a washstand and a couple of chairs beside it. A neat carpet covered the floor, and the window was screened by a shade.

"You see it is pretty good size for a hall bedroom," said the landlady. "There is no closet, but you can hang your clothes on that row of pegs. If there are not enough, I will have some more put in."

"I think there will be enough," said Rufus, thinking, as he spoke, of his limited wardrobe. He was not much better off than the man who carried all his clothes on his back, and so proclaimed himself independent of trunk-makers.

"Well, Rufus, what do you think of the room?" asked Miss Manning.

"I'll take it," said our hero, promptly. He had been on the point of calling it *bully*, when it occurred to him that perhaps such a word might not be the most appropriate under the circumstances.

"When will you come, Mr. ——?" here the landlady hesitated, not having been made acquainted with the last name of our new boarder. Here it occurs to me that as yet our hero has not been introduced by his full name, although this is the second volume of his adventures. It is quite time that this neglect was remedied.

"Rushton," said Rufus.

"When will you take possession of the room, Mr. Rushton?"

"I'll be here to-night to dinner," said Rufus, "Maybe I won't send my trunk round till to-morrow."

"I didn't know you had a trunk, Rufie," said Rose, innocently.

"I don't carry my trunk round all the time like an elephant, Rosy," said her brother, a little embarrassed by his sister's revelation, for he wanted to keep up appearances in his new character as a boarder at an up-town boarding-house.

"Rufus, wouldn't you like to go up and see my room?" interposed Miss Manning; "it's on the next floor, but, though rather high up, I think you will like it."

This opportune interruption prevented Rose from making any further reference to the trunk.

So they proceeded upstairs.

Though Mr. Colman had not yet sent in the additional furniture promised by his wife, the room was looking bright and pleasant. The carpet had a rich, warm tint, and everything looked, as the saying is, as neat as a pin.

"This is to be my room," said Miss Manning, with satisfaction,—"my room and Rosy's. I hope you will often come up to visit us. How do you like it?"

"Bully," said Rufus, admiringly, unconsciously pronouncing the forbidden word.

"I think we shall be very comfortable here," said Miss Manning.

Here a child's step was heard upon the stairs, and Jennie Colman entered.

"Mamma would like to see you downstairs, Miss Manning," she said.

"Good-morning, my dear," said her new governess. "Rufus, this is one of my pupils."

"Is that your husband, Miss Manning?" asked Jennie, surveying Rufus with attention.

Rufus laughed, and Miss Manning also.

"He would be rather a young husband for me, Jennie," she said. "He is more suitable for you."

"I am not old enough to be married yet," she answered, gravely; "but perhaps I will marry him some time. I like his looks."

Rufus blushed a little, not being in the habit of receiving compliments from young ladies.

"Have you got that doll for me, Jennie?" asked Rose, introducing the subject which had the greatest interest for her.

"Yes, I've got it downstairs, in mamma's room."

They went down, and at the door of Mrs. Colman's room Miss Manning said, "Won't you come in, Rufus? I will introduce you to Mrs. Colman."

"Yes, come in," said Jennie, taking his hand.

But Rufus declined, feeling bashful about being introduced.

"It's time for me to go to the office," he said; "some other time will do."

"You'll be here in time for dinner, Rufus?"

"Yes," said our hero, and putting on his hat he made his escape, feeling considerably relieved when he was fairly in the open air.

"I s'pose I'll get used to it after a while," he said to himself.

"I am glad you have come, Miss Manning," said Mrs. Colman, extending her hand. "You will be able to relieve me of a great deal of my care. The children are good, but full of spirits, and when I have one of my nervous headaches, the noise goes through my head like a knife. I hope you won't find them a great deal of trouble."

"I don't anticipate that," said the new governess, cheerfully; "I am fond of children."

"Do you ever have the headache?"

"Very seldom."

"Then you are lucky. Children are a great trial at such a time."

"Have you the headache this morning, Mrs. Colman?" asked Miss Manning, in a tone of sympathy.

"Not badly, but I am seldom wholly free from it. Now suppose we talk a little of our plans. It is time the children were beginning to learn to read. Can your little girl read?"

"A little; not very much."

"I suppose it will be better not to require them to study more than an hour or two a day, just at first. The rest of the time you can look after them. I am afraid you will find it quite an undertaking."

"I am not afraid of that," said Miss Manning, cheerfully.

"The children have no books to study from. Perhaps you had better take them out for a walk now, and stop on your way at some Broadway bookseller's, and get such books as you think they will need."

"Very well."

"Are we going out to walk?" said Jennie. "I shall like that."

"And I too," said Carrie.

"I hope you won't give Miss Manning any trouble," said their mother. "Here is some money to pay for the books;" and she handed the new governess a five-dollar bill.

The children were soon ready, and their new governess went on with them. She congratulated herself on the change in her mode of life. When solely dependent on her labors as a seamstress, she had been compelled to sit hour after hour, from early morning until evening, sewing steadily, and then only earned enough to keep soul and body together. What wonder if she became thin, and her cheek grew pale, losing the rosy tint which it wore, when as a girl she lived among the hills of New England! Better times had come to her at length. She would probably be expected to spend considerable time daily out of doors, as her pupils were too young to study much or long at a time. It was a blessed freedom, so she felt, and she was sure that she should enjoy the society of the two little girls, having a natural love for children. She did not expect to like them as well as Rose, for Rose seemed partly her own child, but she didn't doubt that she should ere long become attached to them.

Then, again, she would not only enjoy an agreeable home, but for the first time would receive such compensation for her services as to be quite at ease in her pecuniary circumstances. Five dollars a week might not be a large sum to a lady with expensive tastes; but Miss Manning had the art of appearing well dressed for a small sum, and, as she made her own clothes, she estimated that three dollars a week would clothe both, and enable her to save two dollars weekly, or a hundred dollars a year. This was indeed a bright prospect to one who had been engaged in a hand-to-hand struggle with poverty for the last five years.

She went into a Broadway bookstore, and purchased primers for her new pupils, and a more advanced reading-book for Rose. At the end of an hour they returned home. They found an express wagon at the door. Two men were lifting out a sofa and a rocking-chair.

"They are for your room, Miss Manning," said Jennie. "I heard ma tell pa this morning, to stop at a furniture place and buy them."

Mr. Colman had certainly been prompt, for, though it was still early, here they were.

When they were carried upstairs, and placed in her room, Miss Manning looked about her with pardonable pride and satisfaction. Though the room was on the fourth floor, it looked quite like a parlor. She felt that she should take great comfort in so neat and pleasant a room. It was a great contrast to her dull, solitary, laborious life in the shabby room, for which, poor as it was, she oftentimes found it difficult to provide the weekly rent.

There were no lessons that morning, for Miss Manning had her trunk to unpack, and Rose's clothes and her own to lay away in the bureau-drawers. She had about completed this work when the bell rang for lunch. Taking Rose by the hand, she led her downstairs to the basement, where, as is common in New York boarding-houses, the dining-room was situated.

There were five ladies and children at the table, the gentlemen being obliged, on account of the distance, to take their lunch down town, somewhere near their places of business.

"You may take this seat, Miss Manning," said the landlady, indicating one near herself. "Your little girl can sit between us, and Jennie and Carrie on the other side. I will trouble you to take care of them. Their mother seldom comes down to lunch."

The repast was plain but plentiful, the principal meal, dinner, being at six, an hour more convenient for men of business. I state this for the benefit of those of my readers who live in the country, and are accustomed to take dinner in the middle of the day.

Miss Manning was introduced to Mrs. Pratt, a stout, elderly lady, with a pleasant face, who sat opposite her; to Mrs. Florence, a young lady recently married, who sat at her left; and to Mrs. Clifton, formerly Miss Peyton, who, as well as her husband, will be remembered by the readers of the second and third volumes of this series. Mr. Clifton kept a dry goods store on Eighth Avenue.

In the afternoon, Miss Manning gave her first lesson, and succeeded in interesting her young pupils, who proved quite docile, and seemed to have taken a fancy to their new governess.

Meanwhile Rufus had succeeded in making an arrangement which promised to add to his weekly income. Of this an account will be given in the next chapter.

CHAPTER VII

A NEW ENTERPRISE

Rufus felt some doubts as to whether he had done wisely in agreeing to board at Mrs. Clayton's. His own board, together with what he paid for his sister's board and clothes, would just take up the whole of his salary. However, he would have the interest on his five hundred dollars, now deposited in a savings-bank, and yielding six per cent. interest annually. Still this would amount only to thirty dollars, and this would not be sufficient to pay for his clothes alone, not to mention miscellaneous expenses, such as car-fares and other incidental expenses. He felt that he should like now and then to go on an excursion with his sister and Miss Manning, or perhaps to a place of amusement. For all this, one hundred dollars a year would be needed, at a moderate calculation. How should he make up this amount?

Two ways suggested themselves to Rufus. One was, draw upon his principal. Probably he would not be obliged to do this very long, as, at the end of six months, it was probable that his salary would be raised if he gave satisfaction, and this he meant to do. Still, Rufus did not like this plan, for five hundred dollars seemed a good round sum, and he wanted to keep it all. The other way was to make up the necessary sum by extra work outside of the office. This idea he liked best. But it suggested another question, which was not altogether easy to answer. "What should he do, or what kind of work should he choose?"

He might go back to his old employment. As he was not required to be at the office before nine o'clock, why should he not spend an hour or two in the early morning in selling newspapers? He felt confident that he could in this way clear two dollars a week. But there were two objections which occurred to him. The first was, that as Mrs. Clayton's breakfast was at half-past seven in the winter, and not earlier than seven in the summer, he would be obliged to give it up, and take breakfast at some restaurant down town. His breakfasts, probably, would come to very nearly the sum he would make by selling papers, and as Mrs. Clayton took him under her usual price, it was hardly to be expected that she would make any allowance for his absence from the morning meal. Besides, Rufus had left his old life behind him, and he did not want to go back to it. He doubted, also, whether his employer would like to have him spend his time before office hours in selling papers. Then, again, he was about to board at a house of very good rank, and he felt that he did not wish to pass among his new acquaintances as a newsboy, if he could get something better to do. Of course it was respectable, as all honest labor is; but our hero felt that by this time he was suited to something better.

The more Rufus balanced these considerations in his mind, the more perplexed he became. Meanwhile he was walking down Broadway on his way to the office.

Just as he was crossing Canal Street, some one tapped him on the shoulder. Turning round, he recognized a young man whom he remembered as clerk in a stationery store in Nassau Street. His name was George Black.

"Rough and Ready!" he exclaimed, in surprise. "Is this you? Why are you not selling papers? You got up late this morning, didn't you?"

"I've given up selling papers," said Rufus.

"How long since?"

"Only a few days."

"What are you up to now?"

"I'm in an office in Wall Street."

"What sort of an office?"

"A banker's,—Mr. Turner's."

"Yes, I know the firm. What do you get?"

"Eight dollars a week."

"That's pretty good,—better than selling papers."

"Yes, I like it better, though I don't make any more money than I did before. But it seems more like business."

"Well, you've found a place, and I've lost one."

"How is that?"

"My employer failed, and the business has gone up," said Black.

"I suppose you are looking for a new place."

"Yes; but I wouldn't if I only had a little capital."

"What would you do then?"

"I was walking up Sixth Avenue yesterday, when I saw a neat little periodical and fancy goods store for sale, on account of the owner's illness. It's a very good location, and being small does not require much capital to carry it on. The rent is cheap,—only twenty dollars a month. By adding a few articles, I could make a thousand dollars a year out of it."

"Why don't you take it?"

"Because I haven't got but a hundred dollars in the world, and I expect that will be gone before I get a new place."

"What does the owner want for his stock?"

"He says it cost him seven hundred dollars; but he's sick, and wants to dispose of it as soon as possible. He'll sell out for five hundred dollars cash."

"Are you sure the stock is worth that much?" asked Rufus.

"Yes, I am sure it is worth more. I've been in the business, and I can judge."

"Why don't you borrow the money?"

"It is easy enough to say that, but where shall I find anybody to lend it?"

"You might take a partner with money."

"So I might, if I could find one."

"Look here, Mr. Black," said Rufus, in a businesslike tone, "what offer will you make to any one who will furnish you the money to buy out this shop?"

"Do you know of anybody who has got the money?" asked the young man.

"Perhaps I do, and perhaps I don't; but maybe I might find somebody."

"I'll tell you what I'll do. If any one will set me up there, I will give him a third of the profits after paying expenses."

"And you think that you can make a thousand dollars a year?"

"Yes, I feel sure of it."

"That's a good offer," said Rufus, meditatively.

"I'm willing to make it. At that rate I shall make fourteen dollars a week, and I have never been paid but twelve for clerking it. Besides, I should be my own master."

"You might not make so much."

"If I make less I can live on less. There's a small room in back, where I can put in a bed, that will save me room-rent. My meals I can buy at the restaurants. I don't believe it will cost me over three hundred and fifty dollars to live."

"So that you could save up money."

"Yes, I should be sure to. After a while I could buy out the whole business."

Rufus was silent for a moment. He had five hundred dollars. Why should he not set up George Black in business on the terms proposed? Then, instead of getting a paltry thirty dollars' interest for his money, he would get two or three hundred dollars, and this would abundantly make up what he needed to live in good style at Mrs. Clayton's, and afford Rose and himself occasional recreation. Of course a good deal depended on the honesty of George Black. But of this young man Rufus had a very good opinion, having known him for two or three years. Besides, as partner he would be entitled to inquire into the state of the business at any time, and if anything was wrong he would take care that it was righted.

"What are you thinking about?" inquired the young man, observing his silence.

"How would you like me for a partner?" asked Rufus, looking up suddenly.

"I'd just as lief have you as anybody, if you had the money," said George Black.

"I have got the money," said our hero.

"You don't mean to say you've got five hundred dollars?" asked Black, in surprise.

"Yes, I do."

"How did you get it? You didn't make it selling papers in the street."

"You may bet on that. No; I found part of it and the rest I had given me."

"Tell me about it."

Rufus did so.

"Where is the money?"

"I keep it in a savings-bank."

"I'll tell you what, Rufus," said George, "if you'll buy out the shop for me, and come in as my partner, I'll do what I said, and that'll be a good deal better than the savings-bank can do for you."

"That's true; but there'll be more risk."

"I don't think there will. I shall manage the business economically, and you can come in any time and see how it's going on. But I never thought you had so much money."

"If you had, maybe you'd have thought more of me," said Rufus.

"Maybe I should. 'Money makes the mare go' in this world. But when will you let me know about it? I've only got two days to decide in."

"I should like to see the shop myself," said Rufus, with commendable prudence.

"Of course; that's what I'd like to have you do. When will you come round with me and see it?"

"I can't come now," said our hero, "for it would make me late at the office. Is it open in the evening?"

"Yes."

"Then I'll tell you what. I'll meet you there this evening at eight o'clock. Just give me the number, and I'll be sure to be there."

"All right. Have you got a pencil?"

"Yes; and here's one of our cards. You can put it down here."

The address was put down, and the two parted.

George Black went round to the shop at once to say that he would probably be able to make an arrangement. In the evening, at the appointed hour, the two met at the periodical store.

Rufus was favorably impressed on first entering. The room was small, but it was very neat. It had a good window opening to the street, and it appeared well filled with stock. A hasty survey satisfied our hero that the stock was really worth more than the amount asked for it.

The proprietor seemed a sickly-looking man, and the plea of ill-health, judging from his appearance, might readily be credited.

"This is the capitalist I spoke of this morning," said George Black, introducing Rufus.

"He seems young,", said the proprietor, a little surprised.

"I'm not very aged yet," said Rufus, smiling.

"The main thing is, that he's got the money," said Black. "He's in business in Wall Street, and is looking about for an investment of his spare funds."

Rufus was rather pleased with this way of stating his position. He saw that it heightened his importance considerably in the mind of the owner of the shop.

"He'll do well to invest here," said the latter. "It's a good stand. I wouldn't sell out if my health would let me hold on. But confinement doesn't suit me. The doctor says I shan't live a year, if I stay here, and life is better than money."

"That's so."

"How long has this shop been established?" asked Rufus.

"Five years."

"It ought to be pretty well known."

"Yes; it's got a good run of custom. If the right man takes hold of it, he'll make money. He can't help it."

"What do you think of it, Rufus?" asked George Black, turning to our hero. "Isn't it as I represented?"

"Yes," said Rufus. "I should think a good business might be done here."

"If I get hold of it, a good business shall be done here," said

Black, emphatically. "But it all depends on you. Say the word, and we'll close the bargain now."

"All right!" said Rufus, promptly. "I'll say the word. We'll take the shop."

CHAPTER VIII

THE NEW BOARDING-HOUSE

It might be considered hazardous for Rufus to invest all his money in a venture which depended to so great an extent upon the honesty of another. But there is no profit without risk, and our hero felt considerable confidence in the integrity of his proposed partner. It occurred to him, however, that he might need some money before he should receive any from the business. Accordingly, as the young man had told him that he had a hundred dollars, he proposed that he should contribute one half of that sum towards the purchase of the shop, while he made up the balance,—four hundred and fifty dollars. This would leave him fifty dollars for contingent expenses, while George Black would have the same.

Our hero's street-life had made him sharp, and he determined to secure himself as far as possible. He accordingly proposed to George Black that they should go to a lawyer, and have articles of agreement drawn up. For this, however, he did not have time till the next morning.

One article proposed by Rufus was, that he should draw fifty dollars a quarter towards the third share of the profits, which it was agreed that he should receive, and at the end of the year any balance that might remain due. No objection was made by George Black, who considered this provision a fair one. The style of the firm,—for as most of the capital was furnished by Rufus, it was thought that his name should be represented,—was "Rushton & Black."

A new sign was ordered, bearing their names, and it was arranged that the new proprietors should take possession of the store at the commencement of the next week, when it would probably be ready.

Rufus hesitated about announcing his new venture to Miss Manning and Rose, but finally concluded not to do so just at present. It would be time, he thought, when they had got fairly started.

Meanwhile he had transferred himself to the room at Mrs. Clayton's boarding-house. He felt rather bashful at first about appearing at the table. Half an hour before the time, he reached the house, and went up at once to Miss Manning's room.

"O Rufie!" said Rose, jumping up from the sofa and running to meet him, "have you come to stay?"

"Yes, Rosie," he answered, sitting down on the sofa, and taking her in his lap.

"I am *so* glad. You are going down to dinner, aint you?"

"Yes, I suppose so."

"We have such nice dinners,—don't we, Miss Manning?"

"Very nice, Rose."

"A great deal better than I ever had before. I wonder where you will sit, Rufie."

"He will sit next to you, Rose; I spoke to Mrs. Clayton about it. Rufus will take care of you, and I am to look after Jennie and Carrie."

"That will be very nice."

"How do you like the little girls, Rose?" asked her brother.

"Very much. They have given me some of their dolls."

"And which knows the most,—you or they?"

"Oh, I know ever so much more," said Rose, positively.

"Is that true, Miss Manning, or is Rose boasting?" asked Rufus.

"Rose is farther advanced than either Jennie or Carrie," answered Miss Manning. "They have studied comparatively little yet, but I find them docile, and I think they will soon improve."

By the time Rufus had combed his hair, and put on a clean collar, the dinner-bell rang. He followed Miss Manning down into the dining-room.

"Good-evening, Mr. Rushton," said Mrs. Clayton. "I am glad to see you."

"His name isn't Mr. Rushton," said Rose. "His name is Rufie."

"It is the first time Rose ever heard me called so," said Rufus, smiling. "She will soon get used to it."

He was rather pleased than otherwise to be called Mr. Rushton. It made him feel more like a man.

"You may take that seat, Mr. Rushton," said the landlady. "Your little sister will sit beside you."

Rufus took the chair indicated.

Next to him was seated a lady of thirty or more, whose hair fell in juvenile ringlets. This was Mrs. Clifton, formerly Miss Peyton, who will be remembered by the readers of "Fame and Fortune." Rufus was introduced to her.

"I am very glad to make your acquaintance, Mr. Rushton," said Mrs. Clifton, graciously. "You have a very sweet little sister."

"Yes; she is a very good little girl," said Rufus, better pleased with a compliment to Rose than he would have been with one to himself.

"I understand you are in business in Wall Street, Mr. Rushton."

"Yes," said Rufus. "I am in the office of Mr. Turner."

"I sometimes tell Mr. Clifton I wish he would go into business in Wall Street. He keeps a dry-goods store on Eighth Avenue."

"Can't remember ever hearing you mention the idea, Mrs. C——," remarked her husband, who sat on the other side, in a pause between two mouthfuls. "There aint much money in dry goods just now, by jove! I'll open in Wall Street, if you say the word."

Mrs. Clifton slightly frowned, and did not see fit to answer the remark made to her. Her husband was not very brilliant, either in business, wit, or in any other way, and she had married him, not from love, but because she saw no other way of escaping from being an old maid.

"Do you know, Mr. Rushton," said Mrs. Clifton, "you remind me so much of a very intimate friend of mine, Mr. Hunter?"

"Do I?" added Rufus. "I hope he is good-looking."

"He's very handsome," said Mrs. Clifton, "and *so* witty."

"Then I'm glad I'm like him," said Rufus.

For some reason he did not feel so bashful as he anticipated, particularly with Mrs. Clifton.

"He's soon going to be married to a very rich young lady,—Miss Greyson; perhaps you know her."

"That's where he has the advantage of me," said Rufus.

"Mr. Clifton," said his wife, "don't you think Mr. Rushton looks very much like Mr. Hunter?"

"Yes," said her husband; "as much as I look like the Emperor Napoleon."

"Don't make a goose of yourself, Mr. Clifton," said his wife, sharply.

"Thank you, I don't intend to. A goose is a female, and I don't care to make such a change."

"I suppose you think that is witty," said Mrs. Clifton, a little disdainfully.

It is unnecessary to pursue the conversation. Those who remember Mrs. Clifton when she was Miss Peyton will easily understand what was its character. It had the effect, however, of putting Rufus at his ease. On the whole, considering that he was only used to cheap restaurants, he acquitted himself very well for the first time, and no one suspected that he had not always been accustomed to live as well. The dinner he found excellent. Mrs. Clayton herself superintended the preparation of dinner, and she was not inclined to undue economy, as is the case with many landladies.

"I'm glad I came here," thought Rufus. "It's worth the difference in price."

As they rose from the table, Mrs. Colman asked Miss Manning, "Is that the brother of your little girl?"

"Yes," answered Miss Manning.

"He has a very good appearance; I should like to have you bring him into our room a while."

Miss Manning communicated this invitation to Rufus. He would have excused himself gladly, but he felt that this would have been hardly polite; therefore he accepted it.

"I am glad to make your acquaintance, Mr. Rushton," said Mrs. Colman.

"Thank you," said Rufus.

"I hear that you have come to board with us."

"Yes," he answered, wishing that he might think of something more to say, but not succeeding.

"It is a pleasant boarding-place; I hope you will like it."

"I think I shall."

"You have a very nice little sister; my little girls like her very much. She will be a great deal of company for them."

"I think she is a very good little girl," said Rufus; "but then I am her brother, so I suppose it is natural for me to think so."

"You are in an office in Wall Street, I am told," said Mr. Colman.

"Yes, sir," said Rufus.

"Whose, may I ask?"

"Mr. Turner's."

"He is an able business-man, and stands high. You could not learn business under better auspices."

"I like him very much," said Rufus; "but then I have not been long in his office."

"I find Miss Manning relieves me of a great deal of care and trouble," said Mrs. Colman (her new governess being just then out of the room). "I feel that I was fortunate in securing her services."

"I think you will like her," said Rufus. "She is very kind to Rose. I don't know what I should do with little sister, if I did not have her to look after her."

"Then your mother is not living, Mr. Rushton."

"No," said Rufus; "she has been dead for two years."

"And you are the sole guardian of your little sister?"

"Yes, ma'am."

After half an hour's call, which Rufus found less embarrassing and more agreeable than he anticipated, he excused himself, and went upstairs.

On Tuesday of the nest week, he decided to reveal his new plans to Miss Manning. Accordingly, he managed to reach home about half-past four in the afternoon, and invited her and Rose to take a walk with him.

"Where shall we walk?" she asked.

"Over to Sixth Avenue," said Rufus. "I want to show you a store there."

Miss Manning soon got ready, and the three set out.

It was not far,—scarcely ten minutes' walk. When they arrived opposite the store, Rufus pointed over to it.

"Do you see that periodical store?" he asked.

"Yes," said Miss Manning.

"How do you like it?"

"Why do you ask?" she inquired, puzzled.

"Look at the sign," he answered.

"Rushton & Black," read Miss Manning. "Why, that is your name!"

"And I am at the head of the firm," said Rufus complacently.

"What does it all mean?" asked Miss Manning. "How can it be?"

"I'll tell you," said Rufus.

A few words made her understand.

"Now," said Rufus, "let us go over to *my* store, and look in."

"What, is it your store, Rufie?" asked Rose.

"Yes, little sister, it's part mine."

When they entered, they found George Black behind the counter, waiting on a customer, who directly went out.

"Well, George, how's business?" asked Rufus.

"It opens well," said his partner, cheerfully. "It's a good stand, and there's a good run of custom."

"This is my friend, Miss Manning," said Rufus, "and my little sister Rose."

"I am glad to see you, Miss Manning," said the young man. "I hope," he added, smiling, "you will give us a share of your patronage."

"We'll buy all our slate-pencils at Rufie's store, won't we, Miss Manning?" said Rose.

"Yes, I think so," answered Miss Manning, with a smile.

"Then," said Rufus, "we shall be certain to succeed, if there's a large profit on slate-pencils, George."

"Yes, if you charge high enough."

After a little more conversation they left the store.

"What do you think of my store, Miss Manning?" asked Rufus.

"It's a very neat one. I had no idea you had become so extensive a business-man, Rufus."

"Is Rufie an extensive man?" asked Rose.

"I hope to be some day," said Rufus, smiling.

CHAPTER IX

AT THE END OF THREE MONTHS

Rufus soon became accustomed to his new boarding-house, and came to like it. It gratified his pride to perceive that he was regarded as an equal by his fellow-boarders, and that his little sister Rose was a general favorite. It seemed almost a dream, and a very disagreeable one, the life they had formerly lived in the miserable tenement-house in Leonard Street; but still the remembrance of that time heightened his enjoyment of his present comforts and even luxuries. He usually spent the evening in Miss Manning's room, and, feeling the deficiencies in his education, commenced a course of study and reading. He subscribed to the Mercantile Library, and thus obtained all the books he wanted at a very moderate rate.

By way of showing how they lived at this time, I will introduce the reader to Miss Manning's room one evening, about three months after Rufus had begun to board in the house.

Miss Manning was seated at the table sewing. Her young pupils were gone to bed, and she had the evening to herself. Rufus was reading Abbott's "Life of Napoleon," which he found very interesting. Little Rose had fallen asleep on the sofa.

"What are you sewing upon, Miss Manning?" asked Rufus, looking up from his book.

"I am making a dress for Rose."

"When you get tired, just let me know, and I will sew a little for you."

"Thank you, Rufus," said Miss Manning, smiling, "but I suppose it won't hurt your feelings much, if I doubt your abilities as a seamstress."

"I am afraid I shouldn't make a very good living at that, Miss Manning. Times have changed a little since you used to sew from morning till night."

"Yes, they have. I used to see some hard times, Rufus. But everything has changed since I got acquainted with you and little Rose. I sometimes am tempted to regard you as my good angel."

"Thank you, I don't know much about angels, but I'm afraid I don't look much like one. They never have red cheeks, and do business in Wall Street, do they?"

"From what I have heard, I don't believe Wall Street is a favorite resort with them. But, seriously, everything seems to have prospered since I met you. Really, I am beginning to be a capitalist. How much money do you think I have saved up out of the three dollars a week which you pay me?"

"You've bought some things for yourself and Rose, haven't you?"

"Yes, we have each had a dress, and some little things."

"Then I don't see how you could save up much."

"I made the dresses myself, and that was a great saving. Let me see, you've paid me forty-two dollars, in all, for fourteen weeks. I will see how much I have left."

She went to the bureau, and took out her pocket-book.

"I have twenty-five dollars," she said, counting the contents. "Am I not growing rich?"

"Perhaps you'd like to speculate with it in Wall Street?" suggested Rufus.

"I think I'd better keep the money, or put it in a savings-bank."

"When you have money enough, I can buy you a fifty-dollar government bond."

"I shall have to wait a while first."

"Well, as for me," said Rufus, "I can't tell exactly how I do stand. I took fifty dollars out of that five hundred I had in the savings-bank. I think I've got about half of it left. The rest of it went for a trunk, car fare, and other expenses. So, you see, I've been going down hill, while you've been climbing up."

"Have you drawn anything from your store yet, Rufus? You were to draw fifty dollars a quarter, I believe."

"Yes; and that reminds me that George Black promised to call this evening, and pay the money. It's about time to expect him."

Rufus had hardly spoken, when a servant knocked at the door.

Rufus opened it.

"There's a young man downstairs, that would like to see you, Mr. Rushton," she said.

"Where is he, Nancy?"

"In the parlor."

"I'll go right down. I think it must be Black," he said, turning to Miss Manning.

"If it is, of course you will bring him up."

"Yes, I should like to. We can't talk very well in such a public place."

Rufus went down, and shortly reappeared with George Black.

"Good-evening, Mr. Black," said Miss Manning; "take a seat. I hope you are well."

"I'm thriving," said Black. "How pleasant and cheerful you look!"

"Yes, the room is rather high up; but it is pleasant when you get to it."

"We were just speaking of you, when the girl came to let us know that you were here."

"I hope you said nothing very bad about me."

"Not very."

"I think I shall be welcome, as I have brought you some money."

"Money is always welcome here," said Rufus. "I'll take care of all you can bring."

"I have brought fifty dollars, according to our agreement."

"Can you spare that amount without affecting the business?"

"Oh, yes."

"I suppose you can't tell me what the profits have been for the last three months."

"Not exactly; but I have made a rough calculation. As it was the first quarter, I knew you would like to know."

"Well, what is your estimate?"

"As well as I can judge we have cleared about two hundred and fifty dollars."

"That is at the rate of a thousand dollars a year."

"Yes; isn't that doing well?"

"Capitally. Do you think the business will hold out at that rate?"

"I feel sure of it. I hope to improve upon it."

"Even if you don't, that will give you nearly seven hundred dollars a year, and me over three hundred."

"That's better than clerking,—for me, I mean."

"Perhaps you might get more as a clerk."

"Perhaps I might; but now I am my own master, and then I shouldn't be. Besides, I have plans in view which I think will increase our custom, and of course our profits also."

"Success to the firm of Rushton & Black!" said Miss Manning, smiling.

"Thank you," said Rufus; "I like that sentiment, and I'd drink to it if I saw anything to drink. Have you got any champagne in the closet, Miss Manning?"

"All that I ever had there, Rufus. If a glass of water will do as well, I can give you that."

At this moment a knock was heard at the door. Miss Manning

rose and opened it. The visitor proved to be Mrs. Clifton, of whom mention has already been made.

"Good-evening, Mrs. Clifton," said the governess; "come in."

"Thank you, but I didn't know you had company."

"Don't stand on ceremony, Mrs. Clifton," said Rufus; "my friend, Mr. Black, is perfectly harmless, I assure you. He is neither a bull nor a bear."

"What spirits you have, Mr. Rushton!"

"No spirits at all, Mrs. Clifton. Miss Manning has just been offering us some water as a substitute."

"You are *so* lively, Mr. Rushton. You remind me so much of my friend, Mr. Hunter."

"I suppose he was one of your admirers before you became Mrs. Clifton."

"Really, Mr. Rushton, you mustn't say such things. Mr. Hunter and I were very intimate friends, but nothing more, I assure you."

"Is Mr. Clifton well?" asked Miss Manning.

"He hasn't got home from the store. You know the dry goods stores always keep open late. Really, I might as well have no husband at all, it is so late when Mr. Clifton gets home, and then he is so sleepy that he can't keep his eyes open."

It was generally believed that Mr. and Mrs. Clifton did not live together as happily as they might have done,—a fact that will not at all surprise those who are familiar with their history before their marriage, which was quite a business arrangement. Mrs. Clifton married because she did not want to be an old maid, and Mr. Clifton because he knew his prospective wife had money, by means of which he could establish himself in business.

"Are you in business in Wall Street, Mr. Black?" inquired Mrs. Clifton.

"No; I keep a store on Sixth Avenue."

"Indeed! my husband keeps a dry goods store on Eighth Avenue."

"Mine is a periodical and fancy goods store. Mr. Rushton here is my partner."

"Indeed, Mr. Rushton, I am surprised to hear that. You have not left Wall Street, have you?"

"No; I have only invested a portion of my extensive capital. My friend Black carries on the business."

Thus far, Rufus had said nothing in the house about his connection with the Sixth Avenue store; but now that it was no longer an experiment he felt that there was no objection to doing so. Mrs. Clifton, who liked to retail news, took care to make it known in the house, and the impression became general that Rufus was a young man of property. Mr. Pratt, who was an elderly man, rather given to prosy dissertations upon public affairs, got into the habit of asking our hero's opinion upon the financial policy of the government, to which, when expressed, he used to listen with his head a little on one side, as though the words were those of an oracle. This embarrassed Rufus a little at first; but as during the day he was in a situation to hear considerable in reference to this subject, he was generally able to answer in a way that was regarded as satisfactory.

"That young man," remarked Mr. Pratt to his wife in private, "has got a head upon his shoulders. He knows what's what. Depend upon it, if he lives long enough, he will become a prominent man."

"I can't judge of that," said good-natured Mrs. Pratt; "but he's a very agreeable young man, I am sure, and his sister is a little darling."

CHAPTER X

MR. MARTIN AGAIN APPEARS ON THE SCENE

The success of the periodical store put Rufus into good spirits. He saw that it would yield him, if only the present degree of prosperity continued, at least three hundred dollars a year, which would make quite a handsome addition to his income. He felt justified in going to a little extra expense, and determined to celebrate his good luck by taking Martha and Rose to a place of amusement. It happened that at this time a company of Japanese jugglers were performing at the Academy of Music, which, as my New York readers know, is situated on Fourteenth Street.

Meaning it to be a surprise, he said nothing to Rose or Martha, but before going down town the next day, went to the box-office, and secured three reserved seats in an excellent situation. They were expensive; but Rufus was resolved that he would not spare expense, for this occasion at least.

When he reached home at half-past five in the afternoon, he went up at once to Martha's room.

"Miss Manning," he said, "have you any engagement this evening?"

"It is hardly necessary to ask, Rufus," she replied; "my company is not in very great demand."

"You have heard of the Japanese jugglers at the Academy of Music?"

"Yes; Mrs. Florence was speaking of them this morning. She and her husband went last evening."

"And we are going this evening. Wouldn't you like to go, Rosy?"

"Ever so much, Rufie. Will you take me?"

"Yes, I have got tickets: see here;" and Rufus drew out the three tickets which he had purchased in the morning.

"Thank you, Rufus," said Miss Manning; "I shall like very much to go. It is long since I went to any place of amusement. How much did the tickets cost?"

"A dollar and a half apiece."

"Isn't that rather extravagant?"

"It would be if we went every week; but now and then we can afford it."

"You must let me pay for my ticket, Rufus."

"Not if I know it," said Rufus. "It's a pity if a Wall Street banker can't carry a lady to a place of amusement, without charging her for the ticket."

"If you put it that way, I suppose I must yield," said Miss Manning, smiling.

Rose was highly excited at the idea of going to see the Japanese, whose feats, as described by Mrs. Florence at the breakfast-table, had interested her exceedingly. The prospect of sitting up till eleven in the evening also had its charm, and she was quite too excited to eat much dinner.

"Really," said Mrs. Clifton, "I quite envy you, Miss Manning. I tried to get Mr. Clifton to buy tickets, but he hasn't done it."

"First time I heard of it," said her husband.

"You pay very little attention to what I ask,—I am aware of that," said Mrs. Clifton, in an aggrieved tone.

"We'll go now, if you say so."

"We couldn't get any decent seats. When did you buy yours, Mr. Rushton?"

"This morning."

Mrs. Clifton, who was thoroughly selfish, hinted that probably Rose wouldn't care about going, and that she should be glad to buy the ticket, and accompany Rufus and Miss Manning; but this hint failed to be taken, and she was forced unwillingly to stay at home.

To tell the truth, Miss Manning was scarcely less pleased than Rose at the idea of going. Until recently she had been a poor seamstress, earning scarcely enough to subsist upon, much less to pay for amusements. Sometimes in the early evening she had passed the portals of places of amusement, and wished that she were able to break the tedious monotony of her daily life by entering; but it was quite out of the question, and with a sigh she would pass on. Now she was very differently situated, and her life was much pleasanter.

"Can I wear my new dress, Martha?" asked Rose.

"Yes, Rosy. It was fortunate that I got it finished to-day."

"And will you wear yours, too, Martha?"

"Yes, I think so," she said. "Rufus has bought us nice seats, and we must look as well as we can."

When both were dressed, they surveyed themselves with satisfaction. Miss Manning was not above the weakness, if it is a weakness, of liking to appear well dressed, though she was not as demonstrative as Rose, who danced about the room in high enjoyment.

When they were quite ready, Rufus came into the room. He had a pair of kid gloves in his hand, which he twirled about in rather an embarrassed way.

"I can't get the confounded things on, Miss Manning," he said. "I've been trying for some time, but it's no go. The fact is, I never owned a pair of kid gloves before. I'd enough sight rather go without any, but I suppose, if I am going to sit in a fashionable seat, I must try to look fashionable."

Miss Manning soon explained to Rufus how the gloves should go on. This time the success was better, and he was soon neatly gloved.

"They are pretty gloves, Rufus," she said.

"I don't like the feeling of them," said Rufus; "they feel strange."

"That is because you are not used to them. You'll like them better soon."

"I wonder what some of my old street friends would say to see me now," said Rufus, smiling. "They'd think I was a tip-top swell."

Though the gloves did not feel comfortable, Rufus looked at his hands with satisfaction. Step by step he was getting into the ways of civilized life, and he was very anxious to leave as far behind him as possible his street experiences.

Soon after dinner they left the house, and, proceeding to Broadway, walked up as far as Union Square. Then they turned down Fourteenth Street, and a few minutes brought them to the Academy of Music.

The entrance and vestibule were brilliantly lighted. On the steps and in front were a number of speculators, who were eagerly offering their tickets to those who appeared unprovided.

Rufus pushed his way through, with Martha and Rose at his side. His tickets were taken at the gate, but the portion indicating the number of their reserved seats was torn off, and given back to them. On showing them to the usher, they were conducted to their seats, which were in the sixth row from the stage, and fronting it.

"We'll have a good view here, Miss Manning," he said.

Soon the curtain rose, and the performance commenced. To those who have not seen the Japanese in their peculiar performance, it is enough to say that they show marvellous skill and agility in their feats, some of which are so difficult as to seem almost impossible.

All three enjoyed the performance. Miss Manning, though so much older, was almost as much unaccustomed as little Rose herself to such scenes, and took a fresh interest in it, which those who go often cannot feel. Every now and then, little Rose, unable to restrain her enthusiasm, exhibited her delight openly.

I should like, for the benefit of my younger readers, to give a detailed account of some portions of the performance which seemed most wonderful; but my memory is at fault, and I can only speak in general terms.

It was a little after ten when the curtain finally fell.

"Is that all?" asked Rose, half in disappointment.

"That's all, Rosy. Are you sleepy?"

"Not a bit," said Rose, vivaciously; "I should like to stay here an hour longer. Wasn't it perfectly beautiful, Rufie?"

"Yes; it was very good," said Rufus; "I don't know but I like it almost as well as the Old Bowery."

Though he had risen in the social scale, he had not quite lost his relish for the style of plays for which the Old Bowery, the favorite theatre with the street boys, is celebrated. But that he had a suspicion that it was not exactly a fashionable place of amusement, he would like to have taken Rose and Miss Manning there this evening. He would hardly have liked to mention it at the table afterwards, however.

The audience rose from their seats, and Rufus with them. Slowly they moved towards the door, and at last made their way to the entrance. Had Rufus known who was waiting there, he might have felt a little nervous. But he did not know, and it devolves upon us to explain.

Three days before, Mr. Martin, who had been sentenced to the penitentiary for three months, on account of his attempt at picking pockets, which we have already chronicled, was released. To say the least, he left the prison no better than he had entered it. Better in one sense he was, for he had been forced for three months to abstain from drink, and this he felt to be a great hardship. But it had a favorable influence upon his health, and his skin was clearer, and his nose not quite so ruddy as when he was arrested. But so far as good intentions went, he had not formed any during his exile from society, and now that he was released he was just as averse to living by honest industry as before.

However, his resources were still limited. Money had never been very plentiful with him, and just at present he was not encumbered with any. It did not occur to him that the shortest way to obtain some was to go to work; or, if it did, the suggestion did not strike him favorably. It did occur to him, however, that there were charitable persons in the metropolis who might be induced to help him, and he resolved to act upon this suggestion. Accordingly, he haunted the neighborhood of the Academy of Music, until the stream of people began to pour out from it, and then he felt that the time had come for him to carry out his plans.

He went up to a gentleman who was coming out with a young lady leaning on his arm.

"Will you listen to me a minute, sir?" he said, in a whining tone. "I haven't eaten anything since yesterday, and I have no money to pay for a night's lodging."

"Why don't you go to work?" said the gentleman.

"I can't get anything to do, sir. I've been trying for something all day."

The fact was that Mr. Martin had been lounging about a low barroom all day.

"Here, take this, and clear the way."

The gentleman, more to get rid of him than anything else, dropped five cents into his hand, and passed on.

"He might have given a quarter," grumbled Martin; "it wouldn't have hurt him."

He looked up, intending to make a similar application to the next person, when he uttered an exclamation of surprise and exultation. Close before him he saw Rufus and his little sister, accompanied by Miss Manning.

CHAPTER XI

MR. MARTIN'S WILD-GOOSE CHASE

Probably nothing could have given Martin greater pleasure than this unexpected meeting with his step-children. He did not reflect that the pleasure might not be mutual, but determined to make himself known without delay. Hurrying forward, he placed one hand on the shoulder of Rufus, saying, "Glad to see you, Rufus; what have you been up to lately? Here's Rose too, I expect she's glad to see me."

At the first sound of his voice poor Rose began to tremble. Clinging closer to her brother, she said, "Don't let him take me, Rufie."

"He shan't touch you, Rose," said Rufus, manfully.

"You don't seem very glad to see me," said Martin, smiling maliciously.

"That's where you're right," said Rufus, bluntly. "We are not glad to see you. I suppose that don't surprise you much. Come along, Rose."

He tried to leave Martin, but Martin did not choose to be left. He shuffled along by the side of our hero, considerably to the disgust of the latter, who was afraid he might fall in with some acquaintance whose attention would be drawn to the not very respectable-looking object who had accosted him, and learn the relationship that existed between them.

"You seem to be in a hurry," sneered Martin.

"I am in a hurry," said Rufus. "It's late for Rose to be out."

"That's what I was thinking," said Martin. "Considerin' that I'm her natural protector, it's my duty to interfere."

"A pretty sort of protector you are!" retorted Rufus, scornfully.

"You're an undootiful boy," said Martin, "to speak so to your father."

"Who do you mean?"

"Aint I your father?"

"No, you are not. If you were, I'd be ashamed of you. Mr. Martin, we haven't anything to do with each other. You can go your way, and I'll go mine. I shan't interfere with you, and I shan't allow you to interfere with me."

"Ho, ho!" said Martin, "when was you twenty-one, I'd like to know?"

"It doesn't make any difference when. Good-night."

"You don't get rid of me so easy," said Martin. "I'll follow you home."

By this time they had reached the corner of Broadway and Union Square. Rufus was placed in an awkward position. He had no authority to order Martin away. He might follow them home, and ascertain where they lived, and probably would do so. Rufus felt that this would never do. Were their home known to Mr. Martin, he would have it in his power to lie in wait for Rose, and kidnap her as he had done once before. He would never feel easy about his little sister under these circumstances. Yet what could he do? If he should quicken his pace, Martin would do the same.

"What do you want to follow us for?" he asked. "What good is it going to do you?"

"Don't you trouble yourself about that," said Martin, exulting in our hero's evident perplexity. "Considerin' that you two are my children, I may want to come and see you some time."

Here Rose began to cry. She had always been very much afraid of Martin, and feared now that she might fall into his hands.

"Don't cry, Rose," said Rufus, soothingly. "He shan't do you any harm."

"Maybe he won't if you treat him well," said Martin. "Look here, Rufus. I'm hard up—dead broke. Haven't you a dollar to spare?"

"Are you going to follow us?"

"Maybe I won't if you'll give me the dollar."

"I can't trust you," said Rufus, suspiciously. "I'll tell you what," he added, after a little thought; "go up to Madison Park, and sit down on one of the seats, and I'll come up in half an hour, or three quarters at most, and give you the dollar."

"Do you think I'm so green?" sneered Martin. "I might stop there all night without seein' you. All you want is a chance to get away without my knowin' where."

"No," said Rufus; "I'll do what I promise. But you must go up there now, and not follow us."

"That don't go down," said Martin. "You don't ketch a weasel asleep."

"Well," said Rufus, coolly, "you can do just as you please. If you accept my offer, you shall have a dollar inside of an hour. If you don't, you won't get a penny."

Still Martin was not persuaded. He felt sure that Rufus meant to mislead him, and, being unreliable himself, he put no confidence in the promise made by our hero. He prepared to follow him home, as the knowledge of where Rose lived would probably enable him to extort more than a dollar from the fear and anxiety of Rufus. So he repeated:—

"That don't go down! You aint quite smart enough to take me in. I'm goin' to follow you, and find out where you live."

"Better give him the dollar now, Rufus," suggested Miss Manning, who felt nearly as anxious as Rose.

"No," said Rufus, decidedly; "I shan't gain anything by it. As soon as he got the money, he'd follow us all the same."

"What will you do?" asked Miss Manning, anxiously.

"You'll see," said Rufus, composedly.

He had been busily thinking, and a plan had suggested itself to his mind, which he thought offered probably the best way out of the difficulty. He reflected that probably Mr. Martin, judging from his appearance, was penniless, or nearly so. He therefore decided to jump on board a horse-car, and thus elude him.

When they reached the corner of University Place, a car was seen approaching.

Rufus hailed it.

"Are we going to ride?" asked Rose.

"Yes, Rose; and now, whatever I do, I want you to keep perfectly still and say nothing. Will you promise?"

"Yes, Rufie."

Rufus exacted this promise, as Rose might unconsciously, by some unguarded exclamation, betray the very knowledge which he was anxious to conceal.

Martin fathomed the purpose of our hero, and determined not be balked. He had five cents which had just been given him out of charity at the door of the Academy, and, though the fare on the horse-cars was one cent more, he thought he might make it do. Accordingly he got into the car after Rufus.

"I couldn't bear to leave such agreeable company," he said, with a leer. "Horse-cars are free, I believe."

"I believe they are," said Rufus.

"I wonder how much money he's got," thought our hero. "I guess I can drain him after a while."

The conductor came along, and Rufus paid for Miss Manning and Rose, as well as himself. Martin was hanging on a strap near by.

"Your fare," said the conductor.

Martin plunged his hand into his pocket, and drew out five cents. He plunged his hand in again, and appeared to be hunting about for the extra penny.

"I declare," said he, "I believe I've lost the other cent. Won't five cents do?"

"Couldn't let you ride under six cents," said the conductor. "It's against the rules."

"I can't see where it is," said Martin, hunting again.

"I'll pay the other penny," said a gentleman sitting near.

"Thank you, sir," said Martin. "Very much obliged to you. I'm a poor man; but it's on account of some undutiful children that I've spent all my money on, and now they begrudge their poor father a few pennies."

He looked at Rufus; but our hero did not see fit to apply the remark to himself, nor, considering that he used to help support Martin, did he feel any particular remorse.

If Martin had been a more respectable-looking object, if his nose had been a trifle less red, and his whole appearance less suggestive of intemperate habits, the remark he had let fall might have stirred some of his listeners to compassion. But no one, to look at him, would wonder much at a want of filial affection towards such a father. So, though he looked round to notice the effect, hoping that he might elicit some sympathy which should take a pecuniary form, he perceived that his appeal had fallen upon stony ground. Nobody seemed particularly impressed, and the hope of a contribution from some compassionate listener faded out.

Rufus was a witness of this scene, and of course it enabled him to fathom Martin's resources. He congratulated himself that they were so speedily exhausted. He did not get out when the car reached Waverley Place, for obvious reasons, but kept on till they came to Bleecker Street. Rose was about to express surprise, but a look from Rufus checked her.

At Bleecker Street he signalled to the conductor to stop. The latter obeyed the signal, and our hero got out, followed not only by Rose and Miss Manning, but, as might have been expected, also by Martin.

"You don't get rid of me so easy," said the latter, triumphantly.

"Don't I?" asked Rufus, coolly. "Are you going to follow me still?"

Martin answered in the affirmative, with an oath.

"Then," said Rufus, coolly, "I'll give you all the following you want to do."

A car bound in the opposite direction was approaching. Rufus hailed it, and it came to a stop.

Martin, who had not been anticipating this move, stopped a moment, staring, crestfallen, at Rufus; but, recovering himself quickly, jumped on the platform, resolved to try his luck.

Rufus paid his fare. Martin didn't volunteer to pay his, but looked steadily before him, hoping that he might escape the conductor's observation. But the latter was too sharp for that.

"Fare?" he said.

"All right," said Martin, plunging his hand into his pocket. Of course he drew out nothing, as he anticipated.

"I declare," he said; "I believe I haven't any money with me."

"Then get off."

"Couldn't you let me off this time?" asked Martin, insinuatingly; "I'm a poor man."

"So am I," said the conductor, bluntly. "You must get off."

"Isn't there any gentleman that'll lend a poor man six cents?" asked Martin, looking round.

But nobody seemed disposed to volunteer assistance, and Martin was compelled reluctantly to jump off.

But he didn't give up yet. The car didn't go so fast but that he could keep up with it by running. It chafed him that Rufus should get the better of him, and he ran along on the sidewalk, keeping the car continually in sight.

"He's running," said Miss Manning, looking out. "What a determined man he is! I'm afraid he'll find us out."

"I'm not afraid," said Rufus. "He'll get tired of running by the time we get to Central Park."

"Shall you ride as far as that?"

"If necessary."

For about a mile Martin held out, but by this time he became exhausted, and dropped behind. The distance between him and the car gradually increased, but still Rufus rode on for half a mile further. By this time Martin was no longer in sight.

"We'll cross over to Sixth Avenue," he said, "so that Martin may not see us on our return."

This suggestion was adopted, luckily, for Martin had posted himself at a favorable place, and was scanning attentively every returning car. But he waited and watched in vain till long after the objects of his pursuit were safe at home and in bed.

CHAPTER XII

MARTIN'S LUCK TURNS

Martin continued to watch for an hour or two, sitting in a door-way. At length he was forced to conclude that Rufus had given him the slip, and this tended by no means to sweeten his temper. In fact, his position was not altogether a pleasant one. It was now past midnight, and, having no money, he saw no other way than to spend the night in the street. Besides he was hungry, and that was a complaint which was likely to get worse instead of better. As for Rufus, Martin had never before seen him so well dressed, and it seemed clear that he was prospering.

"He's an ungrateful young rascal," muttered Martin,—"livin' in ease and comfort, while I am left to starve in the street!"

It would have been rather hard to tell what Rufus had to be grateful for, unless for the privilege which he had enjoyed for some time of helping support his step-father; but Martin persuaded himself that he was ungrateful and undutiful, and grew indignant over his fancied wrongs, as he lay back in discomfort on the stone step which he had selected as his resting-place.

The night passed slowly away, and when the morning light came Martin got up very stiff and sore, and more hungry than ever, and began to wonder where he was likely to get any breakfast. Begging seemed to him, on the whole, the easiest way of getting along; but it was too early for that. After a while, however, the street began to be peopled, and he walked up to a gentleman who was ap-proaching, and, assuming a look which he thought indicative of wretchedness, whined out, "Would you be willing to help a poor man, sir?"

The gentleman stopped.

"So you are poor?" he said.

"Yes," said Martin, "I have been very unfortunate."

"Why don't you work?"

"I can't find any work to do," answered Martin.

"Haven't you got any friends to help you?"

"They've all turned against me," said Martin. "Even my own chil-dren have turned me out of the house to shift for myself."

"How old are your children?" asked the other.

Martin hesitated, for this question was a little embarrassing.

"One of them is sixteen," he said.

"A son?"

"Yes."

"Did you support him, or did he support you?" was the natural inquiry.

"I supported him," said Martin; "but he's an undootiful, ungrateful scamp, and—"

"Then it appears that he has relieved you from taking care of him, and you have only yourself to provide for. It appears to me that you ought to get along better than before."

"If I could get any work."

"What sort of work do you want to do?"

"If I had a few dollars I could set up in some light business."

"You will have to apply elsewhere for the money, my friend," said the gentleman. "To be frank with you, your appearance doesn't speak in your favor;" and he walked on.

"That's the way the rich and prosperous treat the poor," soliloquized Martin, feeling that the whole world was in a conspiracy against him. Those who undertake to live without work are very apt to arrive at such conclusions.

Martin concluded, on the whole, that he wouldn't refer to being turned out of his house next time, as it might lead to embarrassing questions.

He approached another gentleman, and began with the same appeal for assistance.

"What's the matter? Can't you work?" was the reply.

"I've had a severe fit of sickness," said Martin, forcing a cough; "and I'm very feeble. I haint had anything to eat for twenty-four hours, and I've got a wife and five little children dependent on me."

"If that don't bring something," thought Martin, "nothing will."

"Where do you live?"

"No. 578 Twenty-Fourth Street," answered Martin, glibly.

Now the individual addressed was a gentleman of leisure, of a philanthropic turn of mind, and one who frequently visited the poor at their homes. Martin's story seemed pitiful, and he concluded to inquire into it.

"I'm sorry for you," he said. "I'll go round with you and see your family, and see what can be done for them."

This was just what Martin did not want. As the family he spoke of was entirely imaginary, it would only result in exposure and disappointment. Yet he knew not how to refuse.

"I'm much obliged to you, sir," he said. "I'm afraid it would be too much trouble."

"No, I've nothing pressing for an hour. I always like to relieve the unfortunate."

"What shall I do?" thought Martin, as he walked by the side of the benevolent stranger. At length an idea struck him.

"It isn't everybody that would be willing to risk going with me," he said.

"Why not?"

"They'd be afraid to come."

"Why? What danger is there?"

"My third child is 'most dead with the small-pox," answered Martin, with a very dejected look.

"Good heavens! and I might have carried the infection home to my children," exclaimed the stranger, in excitement.

"Then you won't go with me?" asked Martin.

"Here," said the gentleman, producing fifty cents, "here's a little money. Take it, and I hope it'll do you good."

"I reckon it will," thought Martin, as he took the money. "It'll buy me some breakfast and a couple of cigars. That's a pretty good idea, havin' a child sick with the small-pox. I'll know what to do next time anybody wants to go home with me."

As soon as Martin found himself in funds he took measures to satisfy his appetite. He really had not eaten anything since the middle of the day previous, and felt that he could do justice to a substantial breakfast. He walked along until he came to a restaurant where the prices seemed to be reasonable, and went in. Seating himself at one of the tables, he gave his order, and presently a plate of meat and cup of coffee were placed before him. To these he devoted himself with such vigor that they were soon despatched. Still Martin's appetite was not satisfied. Much as he wanted a cigar, the claims of hunger were imperative, and he ordered breakfast to the extent of his resources.

Opposite him at the table sat a man of middle age, with bushy whiskers, and a scar on his left cheek. He wore a loose sack coat, and a velvet vest. His thick, bunchy fingers displayed two large, showy rings, set with stones, probably imitation. He finished his breakfast before Martin, but still retained his seat, and watched him rather attentively. Martin was too busily engaged to notice the scrutiny to which he was subjected. After sitting a while the stranger drew out a cigar, and, lighting it, began to smoke.

This drew Martin's attention. As the flavor of the cigar, which was a very good one, reached his nostrils, he began to feel a regret that he had not reserved a part of his funds for the purchase of a cigar. His opposite neighbor observed his look, and, for a reason which will appear, saw fit to gratify Martin's desire.

"I don't like to smoke alone," he said, drawing another cigar from his pocket. "Won't you have a cigar?"

"Thank you," said Martin, eagerly accepting it. "You're very kind."

"Don't mention it. So you like to smoke. Light it by mine."

"Yes," said Martin; "I like smoking; but I'm a poor man, and I can't afford to smoke as often as I want to."

"Been unfortunate?" said the stranger, suggestively.

"Yes," said Martin, "luck's been ag'inst me. I couldn't get work to do, and my family turned ag'inst me because I was poor. I've got two children living on the fat of the land, but one of 'em refused me a dollar last night, and left me to sleep in the streets."

"That's bad," said the other.

"He's an undootiful son," said Martin.

"Better luck by and by," said the stranger. "Luck'll turn, it's likely."

"I wish it would turn pretty quick," said Martin. "I've spent my last cent for breakfast, and I don't know where I'm to get my dinner."

"The world owes every man a living," remarked the stranger, sententiously.

"So it does," said Martin. "I don't see what's the use of bein' born at all, if you're goin' to starve afterwards."

"Very true. Now I'll tell you what my principle is."

"What is it?" asked Martin, who was becoming interested in his companion.

"If the world owes me a living, and isn't disposed to pay up promptly, I think it's perfectly right for me to collect the debt any way I can."

"So do I," said Martin, though he didn't exactly see the other's drift.

"For instance, if I was starving, and my next neighbor was a baker, and had plenty of bread, the law of self-preservation justifies me in taking a loaf."

"Without payin' for it?"

"Yes; if I haven't got any money to pay. I'm entitled to my share of food, and if others keep it from me, I have a right to help myself, haven't I?"

"That's so," said Martin; "only it's dangerous."

"Of course there is a risk about it; but then there's a risk in starvin', isn't there?"

"I should think there was," said Martin.

"I thought we should agree pretty well. Now tell me what you propose to do. Perhaps I can assist you."

"I don't know what to do," said Martin. "I can't get work. What do you do?"

"I'm in business," said the stranger, evasively.

"Couldn't you give me a chance,—that is, if it aint hard work? I aint so strong as I was once, and I aint fit for hard work."

"Well, perhaps I may be able to do something for you," said the stranger. "If you'll walk with me a little way, we'll smoke another cigar, and talk it over. What do you say?"

Of course Martin accepted the proposal with alacrity. He did not want to go back to his work as a carpenter, having lost all relish for honest industry. He would rather beg, or do anything else for a living. He had a very indefinite idea of the nature of the proposal which was coming, but, whatever it might be, he was not likely to be shocked at it.

"Here, give me your check," said the stranger.

He paid, therefore, for Martin's breakfast as well as his own, leaving that gentleman's fifty cents intact. Martin was not used to such attention, and appreciated it. For the first time he began to think that his luck had really turned.

The two went out into the street together, and were soon engaged in earnest conversation.

CHAPTER XIII

MARTIN MAKES A BUSINESS ENGAGEMENT

Martin was agreeably surprised at the attention paid him by his new friend. There are some who have no difficulty in making friends at first sight, but this had not often happened to him. In fact, there was very little that was attractive or prepossessing about him, and though he could not be expected to be fully aware of that, he had given up expecting much on the score of friendship. Yet here was a stranger, who, to Martin's undiscriminating eyes, appeared quite the gentleman, who had given him a cigar, paid his dinner-bill, and treated him with a degree of attention to which he was unaccustomed. Martin felt that he was in luck, and if there was anything to be made out of his new friend he was determined to make it.

They turned down a side street, perhaps because the stranger's course led that way, perhaps because he was not proud of his new acquaintance.

"So you've had poor luck," he remarked, by way of starting the conversation.

"Yes," grumbled Martin, "you may say that. Things have all been ag'inst me. It's a pretty hard rub for a poor man to get a livin' here."

"Just so," said the other. "What's your business?"

"I'm a carpenter."

"And you can't find work?"

"No," said Martin. "Besides," he added, after a pause, "my health aint very good. Hard work don't agree with me."

He might have said that hard drinking did not agree with him, and this would have been rather nearer the truth. But he was afraid his new friend would offer to find him employment as a carpenter, and for this he was not very anxious. There had been a time when he was content to work early and late, for good wages, but he had of late years led such a shiftless and vagabond life, that honest industry had no more attraction for him, and he preferred to get his living by hook or crook, in fact in any way he could, rather than take the most direct path to a good living by working hard for it.

"What is your name?"

"James Martin. What's yours?"

"Mine," said the stranger, pausing, and fixing his eyes thoughtfully upon Martin; "well, you may call me Smith."

"That aint a very uncommon name," said Martin, thinking he had perpetrated a good joke.

"Just so," said the stranger, composedly. "I've been told so often."

"Well, Mr. Smith, do you think you could help me to some light business that wouldn't be too hard on my health?"

"Perhaps I might," said the other. "What do you think you would like?"

"Why," said Martin, "if I only had a little capital, I could set up a small cigar store, or maybe a drinkin' saloon."

"That would be light and genteel, no doubt," said Smith, "but confining. You'd have to be in the store early and late."

"I might have a boy to stay there when I wanted to go out," suggested Martin.

"So you might," said the other. "There doesn't seem any objection, if you can only raise the capital."

This was rather a powerful objection, however, especially as Mr. Smith offered no encouragement about supplying the capital himself. Martin saw this, and he added, "I only mentioned this. I aint any objection to anything else that's light and easy. Do you think of anything I could do?"

"I may be able to throw something in your way," said Mr. Smith. "But, first, I must ask you a question. Can you keep a secret?"

"Yes," said Martin, "just as many as you like."

"Because the business which I have to propose is of rather a confidential character, and a great deal depends on its being kept secret."

"All right; I'm your man then."

"When I saw you in the restaurant," said Smith, "it struck me that you might answer our purpose. You look as if you could be trusted."

"So I can be," said Martin, pleased with the compliment. "I'll never say a word about the matter. What is it?"

"You shall learn presently,—that is, if my partner thinks we had better engage you."

"Where is your place of business?"

"We will go there. Let us jump into this horse-car."

They had reached Eighth Avenue, and entered a car bound downwards. When the conductor came along, Smith said, "I pay for two," indicating Martin. This was fortunate; for Martin's purse was at a low ebb, his entire stock of money being limited to fifty cents.

They rode some fifteen minutes, at the end of which Smith signalled to the conductor to stop.

"We get out here," he said to Martin.

Martin jumped out after him, and they turned westward down one of the streets leading to the North River.

"Is it much farther?" asked Martin.

"Not much."

"It's rather an out-of-the-way place for business, isn't it?" remarked Martin, observing that the street was lined with dwelling-houses on either side.

"For most kinds of business it is," said his new acquaintance; "but it suits us. We like a quiet, out-of-the-way place."

"Are you in the wholesale business?" asked Martin, whose curiosity began to be considerably excited.

"Something of that sort," answered the stranger. "Ah, here we are!"

The house before which he stopped was a brick dwelling-house, of three stories. The blinds were closed, and it might have been readily supposed that no one lived there. Certainly nothing could have looked less like a place of business, so far as outward appearance went, and Martin, whose perceptions were not very acute, saw this, and was puzzled. Still his companion spoke so quietly and composedly, and seemed to understand himself so well, that he did not make any remark.

Instead of pulling the bell, Mr. Smith drew a latch-key from his pocket, and admitted himself.

"Come in, Mr. Martin," he said.

Martin stepped into the entry, and the door was closed.

Before him was a narrow staircase, with a faded stair-carpet upon it. A door was partly open into a room on the right, but still there was nothing visible that looked like business.

"Follow me," said Smith, leading the way up stairs.

Martin followed, his curiosity, if anything, greater than before.

They went into a front room on the second floor.

"Excuse me a moment," said Smith.

Martin was left alone, but in two minutes Smith returned with a tall, powerful-looking man, whose height was such that he narrowly escaped being a giant.

"Mr. Martin," said Smith, "this is my partner, Mr. Hayes."

"Proud to make your acquaintance, I am sure, Mr. Hayes," said Martin, affably. "I met your partner this mornin' in an eatin'-house, and he said you might have a job for me. My health aint very good, but I could do light work well enough."

"Did you tell Mr. Martin," said the giant, in a hoarse voice that sounded as if he had a cold of several years' standing, "that our business is of a confidential nature?"

"Yes," said Martin, "I understand that. I can keep a secret."

"It is absolutely necessary that you should," said Hayes. "You say you can, but how can I be sure of it?"

"I'll give you my word," said Martin.

The giant looked down upon Martin, and ejaculated, "Humph!" in a manner which might be interpreted to convey some doubt as to the value of Martin's word. However, even if Martin had been aware of this, he was not sensitive, and would not have taken offence.

"Are you willing to take your oath that you will never reveal, under any circumstances, anything connected with our business?"

"Yes," said Martin, eagerly, his curiosity being greater than ever.

There was a Bible on the table. Hayes cast his eyes in that direction, but first said something in a low voice to Smith. The latter drew a small brass key from his pocket, and opened a cupboard, or small closet in the wall, from which, considerably to Martin's alarm, he drew out a revolver and a knife. These he laid on the table beside the book.

"What's that for?" asked Martin, with an uneasy glance at the weapons.

"I'll tell you what it's for, my friend," said the giant. "It's to show you what your fate will be if you ever reveal any of our secrets. Perhaps you don't want to take the risk of knowing what they are. If you don't, you can say so, and go."

But Martin did not want to go, and he did want to learn the secrets more than ever.

"I'm ready," he said. "I'll take the oath."

"Very well, you understand now what it means. Put your hand on the book, and repeat after me: 'I solemnly swear, on the penalty of death by pistol or knife, never to reveal any secret I may have imparted to me in this room.'"

Martin repeated this formula, not without a certain shrinking, not to say creeping, of the flesh.

"Now that you have taken the oath," said Smith, "we will tell you our secret."

"Yes," said Martin, eagerly.

"The fact is," said Smith, in a low voice, "we are counterfeiters."

"You don't say so!" ejaculated Martin.

"Yes, there's a light, genteel business for you. There are all ways of making a living, and that isn't the worst."

"Does it pay pretty well?" asked Martin, getting interested.

"Yes, it's a money-making business," said Smith, with a laugh; "but there's a little prejudice against it, and so we have a very quiet place of business."

"Yes, I see," said Martin.

"You see the world owes us a living," continued Smith, "as you remarked this morning, and if it doesn't come in one way, it must in another."

"Isn't it dangerous?" asked Martin.

"Not if it's carefully managed."

"What do you want me to do?"

"Supply money to our agents chiefly. It won't do to have too many come to the house, for it might excite suspicion. You will come every morning, receive money and directions from one of us, and then do as you are bid."

"How much will you give me?"

"What do you say to a hundred dollars a month?"

"In good money," said Martin, his eyes sparkling with pleasure.

"No, of course not. In money of our manufacture."

Martin's countenance fell.

"First thing I know I'll be nabbed," he said.

"Not if you are careful. We'll give you instructions. Do you accept our terms?"

"Yes," said Martin, unhesitatingly.

"Of course you take a risk. No gain without risk, you know. But if you are unlucky, remember your oath, and don't betray us. If you do, you're a dead man within twenty-four hours from the time you leave the prison. There are twenty men bound by a solemn oath to revenge treachery by death. If you betray our secret, nothing can save you. Do you understand?"

"Yes," said Martin, whose mind was suitably impressed with the absolute necessity of silence. The representations of his new friends might or might not be true, but, at all events, he believed them to be in earnest, and their point was gained.

"When do you want me to begin?" he asked.

"To-day; but first it will be necessary for you to be more decently dressed."

"These are all the clothes I have," returned Martin. "I've been unfortunate, and I haven't had any money to buy good clothes with."

"Have we any clothes in the house that will fit this man?" asked Smith of his confederate.

"I will go and see."

The giant soon returned with a suit of clothing, not very fine or very fashionable, but elegant compared with that which Martin now wore.

"I guess these will fit you," he said. "Try them on."

Martin made the change with alacrity, and when it had been effected, surveyed himself in a mirror with considerable complacency. His temporary abstinence from liquor while at the Island had improved his appearance, and the new suit gave him quite a respectable appearance. He had no objection to appearing respectable, provided it were at other people's expense. On the whole, he was in excellent spirits, and felt that at length his luck had turned, and he was on the high road to prosperity.

CHAPTER XIV

HOW RUFUS SUCCEEDED IN BUSINESS

Very little has been said of Rufus in his business relations. When he entered Mr. Turner's office, he resolved to spare no pains to make himself useful, and his services satisfactory to his employer. He knew very well that he owed his situation entirely to the service which he had accidentally been able to do Mr. Turner, and that, otherwise, the latter would never have thought of selecting an office-boy from the class to which he belonged. But Rufus was resolved that, whatever might have been his original motive, he should never regret the selection he had made. Therefore he exerted himself, more than under ordinary circumstances he would have done, to do his duty faithfully. He tried to learn all he could of the business, and therefore listened attentively to all that was going on, and in his leisure moments studied up the stock quotations, so that he was able generally to give the latest quotations of prices of the prominent stocks in the market.

Mr. Turner, who was an observant man, watched him quietly, and was pleased with his evident pains to master the details of the business.

"If Rufus keeps on, Mr. Marston," he said to his chief clerk, one day, "he will make an excellent business-man in time."

"He will, indeed," said the clerk. "He is always prompt, and doesn't need to be told the same thing twice. Besides, he has picked up a good deal of outside information. He corrected me yesterday on a stock quotation."

"He did me a great service at one time, and I mean to push him as fast as he will bear it. I have a great mind to increase his pay to ten dollars a week at once. He has a little sister to take care of, and ten dollars a week won't go far in these times."

"Plenty of boys can be got for less, of course; but he is one in a hundred. It is better to pay him ten dollars than most boys five."

In accordance with this resolution, when Rufus, who had gone to the bank, returned, Mr. Turner called him. Rufus supposed it was to receive some new order, and was surprised when, instead, his employer inquired:—

"How is your little sister, Rufus?"

"Very well, thank you, sir."

"Have you a comfortable boarding-place?"

"Yes, sir."

"How much board do you pay?"

"Eight dollars a week for both of us, sir."

"That takes up the whole of your salary,—doesn't it?"

"Yes, sir; but I have invested the money I had in a stationery store on Sixth Avenue, and get a third of the profits. With that I buy clothes for myself and sister, and pay any other expenses we may have."

"I see you are a great financier, Rufus. I was not aware that you had a business outside of mine. How long have you been with me?"

"About four months, sir."

"Your services have been quite satisfactory. I took you into the office for other reasons; but I feel satisfied, by what I have noticed of you, that it will be well worth my while to retain your services."

"Thank you, sir," said Rufus.

He was exceedingly gratified at this testimony, as he had reason to be, for he had already learned that Mr. Turner was an excellent business-man, and bore a high reputation in business circles for probity and capacity.

"I intended, at the end of six months," pursued Mr. Turner, "to raise your pay to ten dollars a week if you suited me; but I may as well anticipate two months. Mr. Marston, you will hereafter pay Rufus ten dollars a week."

"Very well, sir."

"I am very much obliged to you, Mr. Turner," said Rufus, gratefully. "I didn't expect to have my pay raised for a good while, for I knew that I received more already than most office-boys. I have tried to do my duty, and shall continue to do so."

"That is the right way, Rufus," said his employer, kindly. "It will be sure to win success. You are working not only for me, but most of all for yourself. You are laying now the foundation of future prosperity. When an opportunity occurs, I shall promote you from the post of errand-boy to a clerkship, as I judge from what I have seen that you will be quite competent to fill such a position."

This intelligence was of course very gratifying to Rufus. He knew that as yet he was on the lowest round of the ladder, and he had a commendable desire to push his way up. He saw that Mr. Turner was well disposed to help him, and he resolved that he would deserve promotion.

When he returned home to supper, he carried to Miss Manning and Rose the tidings of his increase of pay, and the encouraging words which had been spoken by Mr. Turner.

"I am not surprised to hear it, Rufus," said Miss Manning. "I felt sure you would try to do your duty, and I knew you had the ability to succeed."

"Thank you for your good opinion of me," said Rufus.

"I can tell you of some one else who has a good opinion of you," said Miss Manning.

"Who is it?"

"Mrs. Clifton. She said this forenoon, that she considered you one of the most agreeable and wittiest young men she was acquainted with."

"I suppose I ought to blush," said Rufus; "but blushing isn't in my line. I hope Mr. Clifton won't hear of it. He might be jealous."

"He doesn't seem much inclined that way," said Miss Manning.

At this moment Mrs. Clifton herself entered.

"Good-evening, Mr. Rushton," she said. "Where do you think I called this afternoon?"

"I couldn't guess."

"At your store in Sixth Avenue."

"I hope you bought something. I expect my friends to patronize me."

"Yes. I bought a package of envelopes. I told Mr. Black I was a friend of yours, so he let me have it at the wholesale price."

"Then I'm afraid I didn't make anything on that sale. When I want some dry goods may I tell your husband that I am a friend of yours, and ask him to let me have it at the wholesale price?"

"Certainly."

"Then I shall take an early opportunity to buy a spool of cotton."

"Can you sew?"

"I never took in any fine work to do, but if you've got any hand-kerchiefs to hem, I'll do it on reasonable terms."

"How witty you are, Mr. Rushton!"

"I am glad you think so, Mrs. Clifton. I never found anybody else who could appreciate me."

Several days had passed since the accidental encounter with Martin outside of the Academy of Music. Rufus began to hope that he had gone out of the city, though he hardly expected it. Such men as Martin prefer to live from hand to mouth in a great city, rather than go to the country, where they would have less diffi-culty in earning an honest living. At any rate he had successfully

baffled Martin's attempts to learn where Rose and he were board-
ing. But he knew his step-father too well to believe that he had got
rid of him permanently. He had no doubt he would turn up sooner
or later, and probably give him additional trouble.

He turned up sooner than Rufus expected.

The next morning, when on the way from the bank with a tin box
containing money and securities, he suddenly came upon Martin standing in front of the general post office, with a cigar in his
mouth. The respectable appearance which Martin presented in his
new clothes filled Rufus with wonder, and he could not avoid staring at his step-father with surprise.

"Hillo!" said Martin, his eye lighting up with malicious pleasure.
"So you didn't know me, eh?"

"No," said Rufus.

"I'm in business now."

"I'm glad to hear it," said Rufus.

"I get a hundred dollars a month."

"I'm glad you are prosperous, Mr. Martin."

"Maybe you'll be more willing to own the relationship now."

"I'm glad for your sake only," said Rufus. "I can take care of Rose
well enough alone. But I must be going."

"All right! I'll go along with you."

"I am in a hurry," said Rufus, uneasily.

"I can walk as fast as you," said Martin, maliciously. "Seein'
you're my step-son, I'd like to know what sort of a place you've
got."

The street being free to all, Rufus could not shake off his un-
welcome companion, nor could he evade him, as it was necessary
for him to go back to the office at once. He consoled himself, however, by the reflection that at any rate Martin wouldn't find out his
boarding-place, of which he was chiefly afraid, as it might affect
the safety of Rose.

"What have you got in that box?" asked Martin.

"I don't care to tell," said Rufus.

"I know well enough. It's money and bonds. You're in a broker's
office, aint you?"

"I can't stop to answer questions," said Rufus, coldly. "I'm in a
hurry."

"I'll find out in spite of you," said Martin. "You can't dodge me as
easy as last time. I aint so poor as I was. Do you see that?"

As he spoke he drew out a roll of bills (they were counterfeit, but
Rufus, of course, was not aware of that), and displayed them.

Our hero was certainly astonished at this display of wealth on the part of his step-father, and was puzzled to understand how in the brief interval since he last saw him he could have become so favored by fortune, but his conjectures were interrupted by his arrival at the office.

"Turner!" repeated Martin to himself, observing the sign. "So this is where my dootiful step-son is employed. Well, I'm glad to know it. It'll come handy some day."

So saying, he lighted a fresh cigar, and sauntered away with the air of a man of independent means, who had come down to Wall Street to look after his investments.

CHAPTER XV

THE TIN BOX

"I met my dootiful son this mornin'," remarked Martin to his employer, at their next interview.

"Did you?" said Smith, carelessly, for he felt little interest in Martin's relations.

"Yes; he's in business in Wall Street."

"How's that?" asked Smith, his attention arrested by this statement.

"He's with Turner, the banker. He was going to the bank, with a tin box under his arm. I'd like to have the money there was in it."

"Did he tell you there was money in it?"

"No; but I'll bet there was enough in it to make a poor man rich."

"Perhaps so," said Smith, thoughtfully.

"How old is your son?" he inquired, after a pause.

"Fifteen or sixteen, I've forgotten which. You see he isn't my own son; I married his mother, who was a widder with two children; that's the way of it."

"I suppose he doesn't live with you."

"No; he's an undootiful boy. He haint no gratitude for all I've done for him. He wouldn't care if I starved in the street."

"That shows a bad disposition," said Smith, who seemed disposed to protract the conversation for some purposes of his own.

"Yes," said Martin, wiping his eyes pathetically with a red handkerchief; "he's an ungrateful young scamp. He's set my little daughter Rose ag'inst me,—she that set everything by me till he made her believe all sorts of lies about me."

"Why don't you come up with him?"

"I don't know how."

"I suppose you would have no objections if I should tell you."

"No," said Martin, hesitating; "that is, if it aint dangerous. If I should give him a lickin' in the street, he'd call the police, and swear I wasn't his father."

"That isn't what I mean. I'll think it over, and tell you by and by. Now we'll talk about business."

It was not until the next day that Smith unfolded to Martin his plan of "coming up with" Rufus. It was of so bold a character that Martin was startled, and at first refused to have any part in it, not from any conscientious scruples,—for Martin's conscience was both tough and elastic,—but solely because he was a coward, and had a wholesome dread of the law. But Smith set before him the advantages which would accrue to him personally, in so attractive a manner, that at length he consented, and the two began at once to concoct arrangements for successfully carrying out the little plan agreed upon.

Not to keep the reader in suspense, it was no less than forcibly depriving Rufus of the tin box, some morning on his way home from the bank. This might bring Rufus into trouble, while Martin and Smith were to share the contents, which, judging from the wealth of Mr. Turner, were likely to be of considerable value.

"There may be enough to make your fortune," suggested Smith.

"If I don't get nabbed."

"Oh, there'll be no danger, if you will manage things as I direct you."

"I'll have all the danger, and you'll share the profits," grumbled Martin.

"Isn't the idea mine?" retorted Smith. "Is it the soldiers who get all the credit for a victory, or doesn't the general who plans the campaign receive his share? Besides, I may have to manage converting the securities into cash. There isn't one chance in a hundred of your getting into trouble if you do as I tell you; but if you do, remember your oath."

With this Martin was forced to be contented. He was only a common rascal, while Smith was one of a higher order, and used him as a tool. In the present instance, despite his assurances, Smith acknowledged to himself that the plan he had proposed was really attended with considerable danger, but this he ingloriously managed that Martin should incur, while he lay back, and was ready to profit by it if it should prove successful.

Meanwhile Rufus was at work as usual, quite unconscious of the danger which menaced him. His encounter with Martin gave him a little uneasiness, for he feared that the latter might renew his attempts to gain possession of Rose. Farther than this he had no fears. He wondered at the sudden improvement in Martin's fortunes, and could not conjecture what business he could have engaged in which would give him a hundred dollars a month. He might have doubted his assertion, but that his unusually respectable appearance, and the roll of bills which he had displayed,

seemed to corroborate his statement. He was glad that his step-
father was doing well, having no spite against him, provided he
would not molest him and Rose.

He decided not to mention to Rose or Miss Manning that he had
met Martin, as it might occasion them anxiety. He contented himself by warning them to be careful, as Martin was no doubt still in
the city, and very likely prowling round in the hopes of finding out
where they lived.

It was towards the close of business hours that Mr. Marston, the
head clerk, handed Rufus a tin box, saying, "Rufus, you may carry
this round to the Bank of the Commonwealth."

"Yes, sir," said Rufus.

It was one of his daily duties, and he took the box as a matter of
course, and started on his errand. When he first entered the office, the feeling that property of value was committed to his charge
gave him a feeling of anxious responsibility; but now he had become used to it, and ceased to think of danger. Probably he would
have felt less security, had he seen Mr. Martin prowling about on
the opposite side of the street, his eyes attentively fixed on the
entrance to Mr. Turner's office. When Martin saw Rufus depart
on his errand, he threw away the cigar he had in his mouth, and
crossed the street. He followed Rufus closely, unobserved by our
hero, to whom it did not occur to look back.

"It's a risky business," thought Martin, rather nervously. "I wish
I hadn't undertaken it. Ten to one I'll get nabbed."

He was more than half inclined to give up his project; but if he
should do so he knew he would get into disgrace with his employers. Besides, the inducements held out to him were not small.
He looked covetously at the tin box under the arm of Rufus, and
speculated as to the value of the contents. Half of it would perhaps
make him a rich man. The stake was worth playing for, and he
plucked up courage and determined to proceed.

Circumstances favored his design.

Before going to the bank, Rufus was obliged to carry a message
to an office on the second floor of a building on Wall Street.

"This is my opportunity," thought Martin.

He quickened his steps, and as Rufus placed his foot on the
lower step of the staircase, he was close upon him. Hearing the
step behind him, our hero turned, only in time to receive a violent
blow in the face, which caused him to fall forward. He dropped the
box as he fell, which was instantly snatched by Mr. Martin, who
lost no time in making his escape.

The blow was so violent that Rufus was for the moment stunned. It was only for a moment, however. He quickly recovered himself, and at once realized his position. He knew, also, that it was Martin who had snatched the box, for he had recognized him during the instant of time that preceded the blow.

He sprang to his feet, and dashed into the street, looking eagerly on either side for the thief. But Martin, apprehending immediate pursuit, had slipped into a neighboring door-way, and, making his way upstairs, remained in concealment for ten minutes. Not suspecting this, Rufus hastened to Nassau Street, and ran toward the bank, looking about him eagerly for Martin. The latter, in the mean while, slipped out of the door-way, and hurried by a circuitous course to Fulton Ferry, where Smith had arranged to meet him and relieve him of the tin box.

"Have you got it?" asked Smith, who had been waiting anxiously for over an hour.

"Here it is," said Martin, "and I'm glad to be rid of it. I wouldn't do it again for a thousand dollars."

"I hope you'll get more than that out of it," said Smith, cheerfully. "You've done well. Did you have much trouble?"

"Not much; but I had to work quick. I followed him into a door-way, and then grabbed it. When'll you divide?"

"Come round to the house this evening, and we'll attend to it."

"Honor bright?"

"Of course."

Meanwhile Rufus, in a painful state of excitement, ran this way and that, in the faint hope of setting eyes upon the thief. He knew very well that however innocent he had been in the matter, and however impossible it was for him to foresee and prevent the attack, the loss would subject him to suspicion, and it might be supposed that he had connived at the theft. His good character was at stake, and all his bright prospects were imperilled.

Meeting a policeman, he hurriedly imparted to him the particulars of the theft, and described Martin.

"A tall man with a blue coat and slouched hat," repeated the officer. "I think I saw him turn into Wall Street half an hour ago. Was his nose red?"

"Yes," said Rufus.

"He hasn't come back this way, or I should have seen him. He must have gone the other way, or else dodged into some side street or door-way. I'll go back with you."

The two went back together, but it was too late. Martin was by this time at some distance, hurrying towards Fulton Ferry.

Rufus felt that the matter was too serious for him to manage alone, and with reluctant step went back to the office to communicate his loss. A formidable task was before him, and he tried to prepare himself for it. It would naturally be inferred that he had been careless, if not dishonest, and he knew that his formerly having been a street boy would weigh against him. But, whatever might be the consequences, he knew that it was his duty to report the loss instantly.

CHAPTER XVI

MR. VANDERPOOL

Rufus entered the office as Mr. Turner was about to leave it.

"You were rather long," he said. "Were you detained?"

"I wish that was all, Mr. Turner," said Rufus, his face a little pale.

"What has happened?" asked the banker, quickly.

"The box was stolen from me as I was going upstairs to the office of Foster & Nevins."

"How did it happen? Tell me quickly."

"I had only gone up two or three steps when I heard a step behind me. Turning to see who it was, I was struck violently in the face, and fell forward. When I recovered, the man had disappeared, and the box was gone."

"Can I depend upon the absolute truth of this statement, Rufus?" asked Mr. Turner, looking in the boy's face searchingly.

"You can, sir," said Rufus, proudly.

"Can you give any idea of the appearance of the man who attacked you?"

"Yes, sir, I saw him for an instant before the blow was given, and recognized him."

"You recognized him!" repeated the banker, in surprise. "Who is he?"

Our hero's face flushed with mortification as he answered, "His name is Martin. He is my step-father. He has only just returned from Blackwell's Island, where he served a term of three months for trying to pick a man's pocket."

"Have you met him often since he was released?" asked Mr. Turner.

"He attempted to follow me home one evening from the Academy of Music, but I dodged him. I didn't want him to know where I boarded, for fear he would carry off my little sister, as he did once before."

"Did he know you were in my employ?"

"Yes, sir; I met him day before yesterday as I was coming home from the post-office, and he followed me to the office. He showed me a roll of bills, and said he was getting a hundred dollars a month."

"Now tell me what you did when you discovered that you had been robbed."

"I searched about for Martin with a policeman, but couldn't find him anywhere. Then I thought I had better come right back to the office, and tell you about it. I hope you don't think I was very much to blame, Mr. Turner."

"Not if your version of the affair is correct, as I think it is. I don't very well see how you could have foreseen or avoided the attack. But there is one thing which in the minds of some might operate to your prejudice."

"What is that, sir?" asked Rufus, anxiously.

"Your relationship to the thief."

"But he is my greatest enemy."

"It might be said that you were in league with him, and arranged to let him have the box after only making a show of resistance."

"I hope you don't think that, sir?" said our hero, anxiously.

"No, I do not."

"Thank you for saying that, sir. Now, may I ask you one favor?"

"Name it."

"I want to get back that box. Will you give me a week to do it in?"

"What is your plan?"

"I would like to take a week out of the office. During that time, I will try to get on the track of Martin. If I find him, I will do my best to get back the box."

Mr. Turner deliberated a moment.

"It may involve you in danger," he said, at length.

"I don't care for the danger," said Rufus, impetuously. "I know that I am partly responsible for the loss of the box, and I want to recover it. Then no one can blame me, or pretend that I had anything to do with stealing it. I should feel a great deal better if you would let me try, sir."

"Do you think there is any chance of your tracing this man, Martin? He may leave the city."

"I don't think he will, sir."

"I am inclined to grant your request, Rufus," said the banker, after a pause. "At the same time, I shall wish you to call with me at the office of police, and give all the information you are possessed of, that they also may be on the lookout for the thief. We had best go at once."

Mr. Turner and Rufus at once repaired to the police office, and lodged such information as they possessed concerning the theft.

"What were the contents of the box?" inquired the officer to whom the communication was made.

"Chiefly railroad and bank stocks."

"Was there any money?"

"Four hundred dollars only."

"Were any of the securities negotiable?"

"There were two government bonds of five hundred dollars each. They were registered, however, in the name of the owner, James Vanderpool, one of our customers. Indeed, the box was his, and was temporarily in our care."

"Then there would be a difficulty about disposing of the bonds."

"Yes."

"We may be able to get at the thief through them. Very probably he may be tempted to offer them for sale at some broker's office."

"It is quite possible."

"We will do our best to ferret out the thief. The chances are good."

"The thief will not be likely to profit much by his theft," said Mr. Turner, when they were again in the street. "The four hundred dollars, to be sure, he can use; but the railway and bank stocks will be valueless to him, and the bonds may bring him into trouble. Still, the loss of the securities is an inconvenience; I shall be glad to recover them. By the way, Mr. Vanderpool ought at once to be apprised of his loss. You may go up there at once. Here is his address."

Mr. Turner wrote upon a card, the name

James Vanderpool, *No. — West Twenty-Seventh Street*

and handed it to Rufus.

"After seeing Mr. Vanderpool, you will come to my house this evening, and report what he says. Assure him that we will do our best to recover the box. I shall expect you, during the week which I allow you, to report yourself daily at the office, to inform me of any clue which you may have obtained."

"You may depend upon me, sir," said our hero.

Rufus at once repaired to the address furnished him by Mr. Turner.

Another difficult and disagreeable task lay before him. It is not a very pleasant commission to inform a man of the loss of property, particularly when, as in the present case, the informant feels that the fault of the loss may be laid to his charge. But Rufus accepted the situation manfully, feeling that, however disagreeable, it devolved upon him justly.

He took the University Place cars, and got out at Twenty-Seventh Street. He soon found Mr. Vanderpool's address, and, ringing the bell, was speedily admitted.

"Yes, Mr. Vanderpool is at home," said the servant. "Will you go up to his study?"

Rufus followed the servant up the front staircase, and was ushered into a front room on the second floor. There was a library table in the centre of the apartment, at which was seated a gentleman of about sixty, with iron-gray hair, and features that bore the marks of sickness and invalidism.

Mr. Vanderpool had inherited a large estate, which, by careful management, had increased considerably. He had never been in active business, but, having some literary and scientific tastes, had been content to live on his income, and cultivate the pursuits to which he was most inclined.

"Mr. Vanderpool?" said Rufus, in a tone of inquiry.

"Yes," said that gentleman, looking over his glasses, "that is my name. Do you want to speak to me?"

"I come from Mr. Turner, the banker," said Rufus.

"Ah, yes; Mr. Turner is my man of business. Well, what message do you bring to me from him?"

"I bring bad news, Mr. Vanderpool," said our hero.

"Eh, what?" ejaculated Mr. Vanderpool, nervously.

"A tin box belonging to you was stolen this morning."

"Bless my soul! How did that happen?" exclaimed the rich man, in dismay.

Rufus gave the account, already familiar to the reader, of the attack which had been made upon him.

"Why," said Mr. Vanderpool, "there were fifty thousand dollars' worth of property in that box. That would be a heavy loss."

"There is no danger of losing all that," said Rufus. "The money I suppose will be lost, and perhaps the government bonds may be disposed of; but that will only amount to about fifteen hundred dollars. The thief can't do anything with the stocks and shares."

"Are you sure of that?" asked Mr. Vanderpool, relieved.

"Yes, sir, Mr. Turner told me so. We have given information to the police. Mr. Turner has given me a week to find the thief."

"You are only a boy," said Mr. Vanderpool, curiously. "Do you think you can do any good?"

"Yes, sir; I think so," said Rufus, modestly. "The box was taken from me, and I feel bound to get it back if I can. If I don't succeed, the certificates of stock can be replaced."

"Well, well, it isn't so bad as it might be," said Mr. Vanderpool. "But are you not afraid of hunting up the thief?" he asked, looking at Rufus, attentively.

"No, sir," said Rufus. "I'd just like to get hold of him, that's all."

"You would? Well now, I would rather be excused. I don't think I have much physical courage. How old are you?"

"Sixteen."

"Well, I hope you'll succeed. I would rather not lose fifteen hundred dollars in that way, though it might be a great deal worse."

"I hope you don't blame me very much for having the box stolen from me."

"No, no, you couldn't help it. So the man knocked you down, did he?"

"Yes, sir."

"That must have been unpleasant. Did he hurt you much?"

"Yes, sir, just at first; but I don't feel it now."

"By the way, my young friend," said Mr. Vanderpool, reaching forward to some loose sheets of manuscript upon the desk before him, "did you ever consider the question whether the planets were inhabited?"

"No, sir," said Rufus, staring a little.

"I have given considerable time to the consideration of that question," said Mr. Vanderpool. "If you have time, I will read you a few pages from a work I am writing on the subject."

"I should be happy to hear them, sir," said Rufus, mentally deciding that Mr. Vanderpool was rather a curious person.

The old gentleman cleared his throat, and read a few pages, which it will not be desirable to quote here. Though rather fanciful, they were not wholly without interest, and Rufus listened attentively, though he considered it a little singular that Mr. Vanderpool should have selected him for an auditor. He had the politeness to thank the old gentleman at the close of the reading.

"I am glad you were interested," said Mr. Vanderpool, gratified. "You are a very intelligent boy. I shall be glad to have you call again."

"Thank you, sir; I will call and let you know what progress we make in finding the tin box."

"Oh, yes. I had forgotten; I have no doubt you will do your best. When you call again, I will read you a few more extracts. It seems to me a very important and interesting subject."

"Thank you, sir; I shall be very happy to call."

"He don't seem to think much of his loss," said our hero, considerably relieved. "I was afraid he would find fault with me. Now, Mr. Martin, I must do my best to find you."

CHAPTER XVII

DIVIDING THE SPOILS

Martin did not fail to go to the house occupied by his employers, in the evening. He was anxious to learn the amount of the booty which he had taken. He decided that it must be ten thousand dollars at least. Half of this would be five thousand, and this, according to the agreement between them, was to come to him. It was quite a fortune, and the thought of it dazzled Martin's imagination. He would be able to retire from business, and resolved to do so, for he did not like the risk which he incurred by following his present employment.

Martin had all his life wished to live like a gentleman,—that is, to live comfortably without work; and now his wish seemed likely to be gratified. In the eyes of some, five thousand dollars would seem rather a small capital to warrant such a life; but it seemed a great deal to a shiftless character like him. Besides, the box might contain more than ten thousand dollars, and in that case, of course, his own share would be greater.

So, on the whole, it was with very pleasant anticipations that Martin ascended the front steps of the counterfeiter's den, and rang the bell.

Meanwhile Smith had opened the box, and his disappointment had been great when he found the nature of its contents. Actually but four hundred dollars were immediately available, and, as the banker no doubt had recorded the number of the government bonds, there would be risk in selling them. Besides, even if sold, they would produce, at the market price, barely eleven hundred dollars. As to the bank and railway shares, they could not be negotiated, and no doubt duplicates would be applied for. So, after all, the harvest was likely to prove small, especially as Smith had passed his word to divide with Martin.

After a while it occurred to him that, as Martin did not know the contents of the box, he could easily be deceived into supposing them less than they were. He must tell a falsehood; but then Smith's conscience was tough, and he had told a great many in the course of his life.

When Martin was ushered into the room, he found his confederate looking rather sober.

"Have you opened the box?" inquired Martin, eagerly.

"Yes," said Smith, rather contemptuously. "A great haul you made, I must say."

"Wasn't there anything in it?" asked Martin, in dismay.

"Yes, there were plenty of bank and railroad shares."

"Can't we sell them?" queried Martin, whose knowledge of business was limited.

"You must be a fool! We can't sell them without the owner's indorsement. Perhaps you'll call and ask him for it."

"Can't we do anything with them, then?" asked Martin, anxiously.

"Nothing at all."

"Wasn't there nothing else in the box?"

"Yes, there was a government bond for five hundred dollars."

Smith concluded to mention only one.

"That's something."

"Yes, it's something. You can sell it after a while, and bring me half the money."

"Will there be any danger in selling it?"

"None to speak of," said Smith, who was afraid Martin might decline selling it, unless he gave this assurance.

"Wasn't there any money?" asked Martin, disappointed.

"Yes, there was a trifle,—a hundred dollars," answered his unscrupulous confederate, who was certainly cheating Martin in the most barefaced manner.

"Half of that belongs to me," said Martin.

"Of course it does. Do you think I wouldn't treat you fair?"

"No," said his dupe. "I know, Mr. Smith, you're a man of honor."

"Of course I am. I'd like to see anybody say I wasn't. I've left everything in the box just as it was, so you might see it was all right."

He went to the cupboard, and, unlocking it, produced the box, of which he lifted the lid. The certificates of stock were at the bottom. Above them, folded up, was the five-twenty U. S. bond for five hundred dollars, and upon it a small roll of green-backs.

"You see it's just as I say, Martin," said Smith, with an air of frankness. "There's the shares that we can't do anything with, here's the bond, and there's the money. Just take and count it, I may have been mistaken in the amount."

Martin counted the roll of bills, and made out just one hundred dollars. Of course he could not be expected to know that there had been three hundred more, which, together with the other bond, were carefully concealed in his confederate's breast-pocket.

"Yes, it's just a hundred dollars," he said, after finishing the count.

"Well, take fifty of them, and put in your pocket."

Martin did so.

"It aint what I expected," he said, rather ruefully. "If I'd knowed there was so little in the box, I wouldn't have taken it."

"Well, it's better than nothing," said Smith, who could afford to be philosophical, having appropriated to himself seven-eighths of the money, and three-fourths of the bonds. "There's the bond, you know."

"Let me see it."

Smith extended it to Martin.

"When shall I sell it?" asked he.

"Not just yet. Wait till the affair blows over a little."

"Do you think there's any danger, then?" queried Martin, anxiously.

"Not much. Still it's best to be prudent."

"Hadn't you better sell it yourself?"

"Suppose I did," said Smith. "I might take the notion to walk off with all the money."

"I don't think you would," said Martin, surveying his confederate doubtfully, nevertheless.

"No, I don't think I would; but if you sell it yourself, you'll have the affair in your own hands."

"But *I* might walk off with all the money, too," said Martin, who thought it a poor rule that didn't work both ways.

"I don't think you would," said Smith, "and I'll tell you why. We belong to a large band, that are bound together by a terrible oath to punish any one guilty of treachery. Suppose you played me false, and did as you say,—though of course I know you don't mean it,—I wouldn't give that for your life;" and he snapped his fingers.

"Don't!" said Martin, with a shudder. "You make me shiver. Of course I didn't mean anything. I'm on the square."

"Certainly, I only told you what would happen to you or me, or any one that was false to the others."

"I think I'd rather have you sell the bond," said Martin, nervously.

"If I were in your case, I'd be perfectly willing; but the fact is, the brokers know me too well. They suspect me, and they won't suspect you."

"I think I've had my share of the risk," grumbled Martin. "I don't see but I do the work, and you share the profits."

"Wasn't it I that put you up to it?" demanded Smith. "Would you ever have thought of it if it hadn't been for me?"

"Maybe I wouldn't. I wish I hadn't."

"You're a fool, then! Don't you see it's turned out all right? Haven't you got fifty dollars in your pocket, and won't you have two hundred and fifty more when the bond is sold?"

"I thought I'd get five thousand," said Martin, dissatisfied.

"It seems to me that three hundred dollars is pretty good pay for one morning's work; but then there are some people that are never satisfied."

"It wasn't the work, it was the danger. I aint at all sure but the boy saw me, and knew who I was. If he did, I've got to keep out of the way."

"Do you think he did recognize you?" asked Smith, thoughtfully.

"I'm not sure. I'm afraid he did."

"I wish we'd got him in our clutches. But I dare say he was too frightened to tell who it was."

"He aint easy frightened," said Martin, shaking his head. He understood our hero better than his confederate.

"Well, all is, you must be more careful for a few days. Instead of staying in the city, I'll send you to Jersey City, Newark, and other places where you won't be likely to meet him."

"That might do," said Martin; "he's a smart boy, though he's an undootiful son. He don't care no more for me than if I was no kith nor kin to him, and he just as lieves see me sent to prison as not."

"There's one thing you haven't thought of," said Smith.

"What's that?"

"His employer will most likely think that the boy has stolen the box, or had something to do with its being carried off. As he took him out of the street, he won't have much confidence in his honesty. I shouldn't be at all surprised if this undootiful boy of yours, as you call him, found himself locked up in the Tombs, on account of this little affair."

"Do you think so?" said Martin, brightening up at the suggestion.

"I think it more likely than not. If that is the case, of course you won't be in any danger from him."

"That's so," said Martin, cheerfully. "I hope you're right. It would be worth something to have that young imp locked up. He wouldn't put on so many airs after that."

"Well, it's very likely to happen."

The contemplation of this possibility so raised Martin's spirits, that, in spite of the disappointment he had experienced in finding the booty so far below what he had anticipated, he became quite cheerful, especially after Smith produced a bottle of whiskey, and asked him to help himself,—an invitation which he did not have occasion to repeat.

CHAPTER XVIII

RUFUS ENTRAPPED

"Now," said Rufus to himself on the morning succeeding the robbery, "I've got a week to recover that box. How shall I go about it?"

This was a question easier asked than answered. Martin being the thief, the first thing, of course, was to find him; and Rufus had considerable hopes of encountering him in the street some day. Should this be the case, he might point him out to a policeman, and have him arrested at once; but this would not recover the box. Probably it was concealed at Martin's boarding-house, and this it was that Rufus was anxious to find. He decided, therefore, whenever he got on the track of his step-father, to follow him cautiously until he ascertained where he lodged.

He walked the street with his eyes about him all day, but did not catch a glimpse of Martin. The fact was, the latter was at Newark, having been sent there by his employers with a supply of counterfeit money to dispose of, so that our hero's search was of course fruitless, and so he was obliged to report to Mr. Turner the next morning.

"Probably he is in hiding," said his employer. "I don't think you have much chance of meeting him for a few days to come."

"I should like to try," said Rufus. "He won't be content to hide long."

"I have notified the banks and railroad companies of the robbery," said Mr. Turner; "so that it will be impossible to sell the shares. After a while, should we fail to recover them, they will grant us duplicate certificates. I have advertised, also, the numbers of the bonds; and, if an attempt is made to dispose of them, the thief will find himself in trouble. So the loss is reduced to four hundred dollars."

"That is too much to lose," said Rufus.

"That is true; but we are lucky to get off so cheap."

"I hope to get back some of that," said our hero, stoutly.

"Did it ever strike you that there might be some risk encountering this man? If he is driven to bay he may become dangerous."

"I don't think of the danger, Mr. Turner," said Rufus. "I lost that box, and it is my duty to recover it if I can, danger or no danger."

Mr. Turner secretly admired the pluck of Rufus; but he was not a man given to compliments, so he only said, quietly, "Well, Rufus, you shall have the week I promised you. I have no doubt you will do your best. I shall not be surprised, however, if you fail."

So Rufus entered upon his second day's search.

He went up Chatham Street, and explored most of the streets intersecting it, visiting many places which he remembered as former haunts of his step-father. But he was quite off the track here. Martin's employment now was on the other side of the city, near the North River, and he had no longer occasion to visit his old haunts. Besides, he had again been sent over to New Jersey, and did not get back to the city at all till late in the afternoon.

The next day Martin complained of headache, and was permitted to remain at home. He did not think it prudent to be out during the day; but easily solaced himself in his confinement with whiskey and cigars, of which he had laid in a good supply. He was sitting in his shirt-sleeves at the front window, looking through the blinds, which were always closed, when his eyes lighted on Rufus passing on the opposite side of the street.

"He's looking for me," exclaimed Martin to himself, observing that Rufus was looking about him as he walked.

"Who's looking for you?" asked his confederate, Smith, who happened just then to enter the room.

"My undootiful son. Look, there he is," said Martin, nervously. "I wonder if he has heard about my living here."

Smith went to the window, and looked out.

"He looks resolute and determined," said Smith. "We must pull his teeth."

"What do you mean?"

"I mean we must put it out of his power to do you harm."

"How are we going to do that?"

"Wait a minute and I'll tell you."

Smith left the room hastily, and after a brief interval returned.

"I think I'll fetch it," he said.

"What have you done?" asked Martin.

"I've sent Humpy to follow your son. He's to carry him a message from you."

"What do you mean?" asked Martin, alarmed.

"Don't be afraid. It's all right."

"But I don't understand it. I didn't send any message. What was it?"

"I'll tell you. If I'm not mistaken Humpy will bring your son back with him, so that I shall have the pleasure of reuniting parent and child."

"You don't mean to say you are going to bring Rufus here?" said Martin, his lower jaw falling. "You aint going to betray me, are you?"

"Stuff and nonsense! What are you thinking of? All you need understand is, that the boy is getting dangerous. He is following you round as if he meant something, and that must be stopped. I mean to get him into the house, but I don't mean to part company with him very soon."

Smith here briefly detailed the instructions which he had given to his errand-boy. Martin listened with much satisfaction.

"What a head you've got!" he said admiringly.

"I'm generally ready for an emergency," remarked Smith, complacently. "You've got to get up early in the morning to get ahead of me."

We must now follow Smith's messenger, and we shall ascertain that gentleman's plan.

Humpy was a boy of sixteen, very short, in fact almost a dwarf, and, as his name implies, disfigured by a hump. He was sharp, however, and secretive, and, though he could not help understanding the character of the men who employed him, was not likely to betray them. He had a pride in deserving the confidence which he saw was reposed in him.

After receiving the instructions of his principal, he crossed the street, and followed Rufus at a little distance, being particular to keep him in sight. Our hero turned a corner, and so did he. He then quickened his pace and came up with him.

"Was you a-lookin' for anybody in particular?" he said.

"What makes you ask?" said Rufus, facing round upon him.

"Maybe I could help you."

"Perhaps you know who I am after," said Rufus, looking at him steadily.

"You're looking for a man named Martin, aint you?"

"Do you know where I can find him?" asked Rufus, eagerly.

"Yes, I do. He sent me after you."

"He sent you!" repeated our hero, hardly believing his ears.

"Yes; he wants to see you."

"What does he want to see me for?" asked Rufus, inclined to be suspicious.

"There's something he's got of yours that he wants to return," said Humpy, in a low voice, looking around cautiously.

Rufus was more and more astonished. Was it possible that Martin's conscience troubled him, and that he wanted to make restitution? He could hardly believe this, knowing what he did of his step-father. Martin was about the last man he would have suspected of being troubled in any such way.

"Yes, he has got something of mine," he said aloud. "Does he want to return it?"

"Yes, he's sorry he took it. He's afraid you'll set the copps on him."

"So he's frightened," thought Rufus. This seemed to throw light on the new phase of affairs. He had never regarded his step-father as very brave, and now concluded that he was alarmed about the consequences of the theft.

"If he'll return what he took, all right," said Rufus, venturing to make this promise on his own responsibility; "he shan't be touched. Where is he?"

"Not far off," said Humpy.

"Tell him to bring it to me, and I'll give my word not to have him arrested."

"He can't come."

"Why can't he?"

"He's sick."

"Where?"

"In a house near by. He wants you to come and see him."

Rufus hesitated.

"What's the matter with him?" he asked.

"He caught a cold, and is threatened with a fever," said the boy, glibly. "If you want to see him, I'll lead you where he is."

"All right! Go ahead!" said Rufus, thoroughly deceived by the boy's plausible story.

"You'll promise not to set the copps on him, after you've got the box?" said Humpy.

"Yes, I promise."

"Then follow me."

Rufus followed, congratulating himself that things were coming out satisfactorily. He had no hesitation in making the promise he did, for he felt sure that he would be sustained by his employer. At any rate, he determined that, having pledged his word to Martin, nothing should make him break it.

Humpy stumped along, followed by Rufus. They turned the corner again, and the boy guided him at once to the counterfeiter's den.

"He's in there," said Humpy, with a jerk of his forefinger. "Come along!"

He mounted the steps, and opened the door, which had been left unlocked.

"He's upstairs," said Humpy. "Come up."

Rufus, without suspicion, followed his humpbacked guide up the narrow staircase. They had scarcely reached the top, when Smith, coming out of a room on the floor below, locked the outer door, and put the key in his pocket. This Rufus did not see, or it would have aroused his suspicion. The boy opened the door of a chamber at the head of the staircase. "Go in there," he said.

Rufus entered, and looked around him, but saw no one. He did not have to wait long. A step was heard at the door, and James Martin entered the room, apparently in perfect health.

"I'm glad to see you, Rufus," he said with a triumphant grin. "You've been such an undootiful son that I didn't much expect you'd come to see your sick father."

Rufus sprang to his feet in dismay. The whole plot flashed upon him at once, and he realized that he had walked into a trap with his eyes wide open.

CHAPTER XIX

IN A TRAP

Our hero's first impulse, on finding himself entrapped, was to escape. He sprang towards the door, but Martin quickly grasped him by the arm, and forced him back.

"No you don't!" he said, with emphasis. "I want you to stay with me."

"Let me go!" exclaimed Rufus, struggling to escape.

"Sorry I couldn't oblige you," said Martin, with a grin. "Can't you stay with your sick father a few days?"

"You've played me a mean trick," said Rufus, indignantly.

"What was you walkin' through this street for?" asked Martin. "Wasn't it because you wanted to see me?"

"Yes," answered our hero.

"Well, you've got what you wanted," said Martin, smiling maliciously. "I know'd you'd never find me if I didn't send out for you. Was there anything partic'lar you wish to say to me?"

"Yes," said Rufus, bluntly. "I want you to give me back that tin box you stole from me the other day."

"What do I know about any tin box?" asked Martin, not knowing that it had been spoken of by Humpy in the street.

"You needn't deny it, Mr. Martin. The boy you sent after me told me you took it."

"He did, did he?" said Martin, seeing that he must try another tack. "Well, s'posin' I did, what then?"

"The law may have something to say. You'll stand a chance of going to Sing Sing for a few years."

"You'd have to prove I took it," said Martin, uneasily. "I only told the boy to say so, so's to get you in here. I read about the robbery in the papers."

"I recognized you at the time, and am ready to swear to you," said Rufus, firmly.

This was rather imprudent, for it made Martin even more determined to prevent our hero's escape.

"If that's your game," he said, "I'll see you don't get a chance to swear to any lies."

"What do you mean to do with me?" demanded Rufus.

"I aint decided yet," said Martin. "Your health's so delicate that I don't think it'll agree with you to go out in the street."

"Are you going to confine me here?"

"Maybe," said his step-father. "I shan't charge you nothing for board. Your cheerful company'll pay me for that."

"Mr. Martin," said Rufus, "I've got a proposition to make to you."

"Go ahead and make it then."

"You've got yourself into a scrape about that tin box."

"I thought you was the one that had got into a scrape," said Martin, jocularly.

"So I have; but mine is of a different kind from yours. You run the risk of going to prison."

"And you're in prison already," said Martin, with a grin. "Seems to me I've got the best of it so far."

"Perhaps you have; but I wouldn't exchange with you for all that. Now I've got a proposition to make."

"That's what you said before."

"If you will restore the tin box, and let me go free, I'll see that you are not arrested for what you've done."

"You're very kind," said Martin; "but that won't pay me for my trouble."

"If I'll get you out of your present danger?"

"I don't know about that. S'posin' I was to do as you say, the first thing you'd do after you got out would be to set the copps on me."

"No, I wouldn't. I'd go to prison first myself."

This proposition had some effect upon Martin. He realized that he was in danger, and felt that he had been very poorly paid for his risk and trouble. He was inclined to believe Rufus would keep his word, but he knew also that matters had gone too far. Smith, he was sure, would not consent to any such arrangement, and without him he could do nothing. Besides, it was a satisfaction to him to feel that he had Rufus in his power, and he had no desire to lose that advantage by setting him free. Tyrant and bully as he was by nature, he meant to gratify his malice at our hero's expense.

"I couldn't do it, Rufus," he said. "There's another man in it, and he's got the box."

Rufus looked sharply at Martin to ascertain if he was speaking the truth. He decided that it was as his step-father stated, and, if this was the case, he would have more than one enemy to deal with.

"Does the other man live here?" he asked.

"Maybe he does, and maybe he doesn't."

"Who is he?"

"Maybe it's the Emperor of Chiny, and maybe it isn't. What would you give to know?"

"Not much," said Rufus, assuming an indifferent tone. "You're the man that took the box,—that's enough for me."

"He put me up to it," said Martin, unguardedly.

"I thought Martin wasn't smart enough to plan the robbery himself," said Rufus to himself. He resolved to appear indifferent to this information, in the hope of learning more.

"You can settle that among yourselves," he said, quietly. "If you consented to do it, you're as much to blame as he."

At this moment Smith, influenced by curiosity, opened the door and entered.

"This is my undootiful son, Mr. Smith," said Martin.

"So his name's Smith," thought Rufus. "I wonder whether it's his real name, or a false one."

"I'm glad to sec you, young man," said Smith. "So you've called to see your father?"

"He isn't my father."

"You see how undootiful he is," said Martin. "He won't own me."

"We'll teach him to be more dutiful before we get through with him," said Smith.

"Mr. Smith," said Rufus, "I'm not here of my own accord. I dare say you know that. But as long as I am here, I'd like to ask you if you know anything about a tin box that was taken from me the other day by Mr. Martin."

"By your father?"

"By Mr. Martin," said Rufus, determined not to admit the relationship.

"What should I know about it?"

"Mr. Martin tells me that, though he took it, somebody else set him to do it. I thought you might be the one."

"Did you say that?" demanded Smith, looking angrily at Martin.

"I was only foolin'," returned Martin, who began to think he had made a blunder.

"It's my belief that you're a fool," retorted Smith. "You'd better be careful what you tell your son. Young man," turning to Rufus, "as to the tin box you speak of, I can tell you nothing. Your father says that he has recovered some property which you stole from him a while since, and I suppose that may be the tin box you refer to."

"That isn't true. It belonged to Mr. Turner, my employer, or rather to a customer of his."

"That's nothing to me. Mr. Martin boards with me, and as long as he pays for his board I don't want to pry into his affairs. If he has taken a tin box from you, I presume he had a better right to it than you had. Are you going to bring your son down to dinner, Mr. Martin?"

"I guess he'd better eat his victuals up here," said Martin.

"Just as you say. I can send Humpy with them. We shall have dinner in about an hour."

"All right; I'll go down now if my dootiful son can spare me."

As Rufus did not urge him to stay, Martin left the room with Smith, taking care to lock the door after him.

"What's the boy's name?" asked Smith, abruptly.

"Rufus."

"He's smart. I can tell that by his looks."

"Ye-es, he's smart enough," said Martin, hesitatingly; "but he's as obstinate as a pig."

"Likes to have his own way, eh?"

"That's what he does."

"He'd make a good boy for our business," said Smith, musingly.

Martin shook his head.

"It wouldn't do," he said.

"Why not?"

"He wants to be honest," said Martin, contemptuously. "We couldn't trust him."

"Then there's only one thing to do."

"What's that?"

"We must keep him close. We mustn't on any account allow him to escape."

"I'll look after that," said Martin, nodding. "I've had hard work enough to get hold of him. He won't get away in a hurry."

"If he does, you'll be arrested."

"And you too," suggested Martin.

"Why should I?"

"Didn't you put me up to taking the box, and haven't you taken half what was in it?"

"Look here," said Smith, menacingly, "you'd better stop that. You've already told the boy more than you ought. If you are taken through your own carelessness, mind what you are about, and don't split on me. If you do, it'll be the worse day's work you ever did. Imprisonment isn't the worse thing that can happen to a man."

Martin understood what his confederate meant, and the intended effect was produced. He began to think that Smith was a desperate man, and capable of murdering him, or instigating his murder, in case of treachery. This made him feel rather uneasy, in spite of his capture of Rufus.

Meanwhile, our hero, left to himself, began to examine the apartment in which he was confined. The door had been locked by Martin, as we have already said. This was the only mode of exit from the apartment, except what was afforded by two windows. Rufus walked to them, and looked out. The room was in the back part of the house, and these windows looked out into a back yard. He could see the rear portions of the houses on a parallel street, and speculated as to the chances of escape this way. As the room was only on the second floor, the distance to the ground was not great. He could easily swing off the window-sill without injury. Though he knew it would not be well to attempt escape now when Martin and Smith were doubtless on the lookout, he thought he would open the window softly and take a survey. He tried one window, but could not raise it. He tried the other, with like want of success. He thought at first that the difficulty lay in their sticking, but, on closer examination, he ascertained that both were firmly fastened by nails, which accounted for their being immovable.

CHAPTER XX

HUMPY

"I might break the window," thought Rufus; but it occurred to him at once that the noise would probably be heard. Besides, if there was any one in the room below, he would very likely be seen descending from the window. If this plan were adopted at all, he must wait till evening. Meanwhile some other way of escape might suggest itself.

The room was of moderate size,—about fifteen feet square. A cheap carpet covered the floor. A pine bedstead occupied one corner. There were three or four chairs, a bureau, and a bedstead.

Rufus sat down, and turned the matter over in his mind. He couldn't make up his mind what Martin's business was, but decided that it was something unlawful, and that he was either employed by Smith, or connected in some way with him. It seemed to him probable that his step-father, in waylaying him and stealing the tin box, had acted under the direction of Smith, and that probably the box was at that very moment in the possession of the superior villain.

"If I could only find the box and escape with it," thought Rufus, "that would set me right with Mr. Turner."

But there seemed little chance of that. It did not seem very probable even that he could escape from the room in which he was confined, much less carry out the plan he had in view.

While he was thinking over his situation, the key turned in the lock, and the door was opened. Rufus looked up, expecting to see Martin; but instead of his step-father there entered the boy already referred to as Humpy.

Humpy carried in his hand a plate of meat and vegetables.

"Here's your dinner," he said, laying the plate down, while he locked the door behind him.

"Look here, Johnny," said Rufus, "you served me a mean trick."

Humpy chuckled.

"You came in just as innocent," he said. "It was jolly."

"Maybe it is, but I don't see it. You told me a lie."

"Didn't you find the man you was after?" said Humpy.

"You told me he was sick."

"So he is. He's in delicate health, and couldn't go to business to-day."

"What is his business?" asked Rufus, a little too eagerly.

Humpy put his thumbs to his nose, and twirled his fingers with a grin of intelligence.

"Don't you wish you knew?" he said tantalizingly.

"Do you know anything about the tin box?" asked Rufus, seeing that his former question was not likely to be answered.

"Maybe I do."

"It's in this house."

"Oh, is it? Well, if you know that, there's no use of my telling you."

"I can't make much of him," thought Rufus. "He's a young imp, and it isn't easy to get round him."

He looked at Humpy meditatively, and it occurred to him whether it would not be well to spring upon him, snatch the key, release himself from the room, and dash downstairs. So far as the boy was concerned, this plan was practicable. Rufus was much his superior in strength, and could master him without difficulty. But, doubtless, Martin and Smith were below. They would hear the noise of the struggle, and would cut off his flight. Evidently that plan would not work. Another suggested itself to him.

"Johnny," said he, "don't you want to make some money?"

Here he attacked the boy on his weak side. Humpy was fond of money. He had already scraped together about twenty dollars from the meagre pay he received, and had it carefully secreted.

"Of course I do," he answered. "How'm I to do it?"

"I'll tell you. That tin box contained property of value. It doesn't belong to me. It belongs to Mr. Turner, the banker. I was trying to recover it when you got me to come in here this morning. Now what I want to say, is this. Get that tin box for me, and help me to get away with it, and it'll be worth fifty dollars to you."

Fifty dollars! Humpy's eyes sparkled when he heard the sum named; but prudence came to his aid, fortified by suspicion.

"Who's a-goin' to pay it?" he asked.

"Mr. Turner."

"S'posin' he don't?"

"Then I will."

"Where'd you raise the money?"

"I'm not rich, but I'm worth a good deal more than that. I'd rather pay it out of my own pocket than not get back that box."

But if Humpy was fond of money, he had also a rude sense of honor, which taught him to be faithful to his employer. He did want the money, and then there was something in our hero's look that made him pretty sure that he would keep his promise. So he put away the seductive temptation, though reluctantly.

"I aint a-goin' to do it," he said, doggedly.

"Perhaps you'll think better of it," said Rufus, who, in spite of the boy's manner, saw the struggle in his mind. "If you do, just let me know."

"I've got to be goin'," said Humpy, and, unlocking the door, he went out, locking it again directly.

Rufus turned his attention to the dinner, which he found of good quality. Despite his imprisonment, his appetite was excellent, and he ate all there was of it.

"I must keep up my strength at any rate," he said to himself; "I may need it."

Meanwhile, as there was no longer anything to dread, Rufus being a prisoner, Martin went out in the service of his employer.

"Now," thought he, reflecting with satisfaction on his signal triumph over Rufus, "if I only knew where Rose was, I'd go after her, and her brother shouldn't get hold of her again in a hurry. He's got enough to do to take care of himself."

This was pleasant to think about; but Martin had not the least

I'll teach you to do it again."

idea where Rose was, and was not likely to find out.

Meanwhile something happened in the counterfeiter's den, which was destined to prove of advantage to Rufus.

Smith sent Humpy out on an errand. The boy was detained unavoidably, and returned an hour later than he was expected. Smith was already in an ill-temper, which the late return of his emissary aggravated.

"What made you so late?" he demanded, with lowering brow.

"I couldn't help it," said Humpy.

"Don't tell me that!" roared Smith. "You stopped to play on the way; I know you did."

"No, I didn't," said Humpy, angrily.

"Do you dare to contradict me, you villanous little humpback?" screamed Smith. "I'll teach you to do it again."

He clutched the boy by the collar, and, seizing a horsewhip, brought it down with terrible force on the boy's shrinking form.

"Let me go! Don't beat me!" screamed Humpy, in mingled fear and rage.

"Not till I've cured you," retorted Smith. Twice more he struck the humpbacked boy with the whip, and then threw him on the floor.

"That's what you get for contradicting me," he said.

The boy rose slowly and painfully, and limped out of the room. His face was pale, but his heart was filled with a burning sense of humiliation and anger against the man who had assaulted him. It would have been well for Smith if he had controlled himself better, for the boy was not one of the forgiving kind, but harbored resentment with an Indian-like tenacity, and was resolved to be revenged.

He crawled upstairs to the small attic room in which he usually slept, and, entering, threw himself upon the bed, face downward, where he burst into a passion of grief, shame, and rage, which shook his crooked form convulsively. This lasted for fifteen minutes, when he became more quiet.

Then he got up slowly, and, going to a corner of the room, lifted up a board from which the nails appeared to have been drawn out, and drew from beneath a calico bag. This he opened, and exposed to view a miscellaneous collection of coins, which he took out and counted.

"Twenty dollars and nineteen cents!" he said to himself. "I've been more'n a year gettin' it. That boy offers me fifty dollars,— most three times as much,—if I'll get him the tin box and help him to escape. I said I wouldn't do it; but he hadn't struck me then. He hadn't called me a villanous humpback. Now he's got to pay for it. He'll wish he hadn't done it;" and the boy clenched his fist, and shook it vindictively. "Now, how'll I get the box?"

He sat on the bed thinking for some time, then, composing his countenance, he went downstairs. He resolved to assume his usual manner, in order not to excite Smith's suspicion.

Smith had by this time got over his rage, and was rather sorry he had struck the boy so brutally, for he knew very well that Humpy might prove a dangerous enemy. He glanced at Humpy's face when he came downstairs, but saw nothing unusual.

"Oh, he'll forget all about it," he thought to himself.

"Here's ten cents, Humpy," he said. "Maybe I struck you too hard. Go and buy yourself some candy."

"Thank you," said the boy, taking the money.

"I've another errand for you."

He told what it was.

"Go and come back as soon as possible."

Humpy went quietly, and returned in good season.

About five o'clock, Martin not yet having returned, Smith directed him to carry up our hero's supper. There was a little exultant sparkle in the boy's eye, as he took the plate of buttered bread, and started to go upstairs.

"So it's you, is it?" said Rufus, on the boy's entrance. "Where is Martin?"

"He aint come in yet. Do you want to see him?"

"No, I'm not particular about it."

Humpy stood looking earnestly at Rufus while he was eating the bread and butter. At length he said, "I've been thinkin' over what you said to me at dinner-time. Shall I get the fifty dollars certain sure if I do what you want?"

"Yes," said Rufus, eagerly. "Get me the tin box, and help me to escape, and the money shall be yours."

"Honor bright?"

"Honor bright."

CHAPTER XXI

SUSPENSE

Rufus generally reached his boarding-house at half-past five o'clock. Sometimes Rose and her two young companions were playing in Washington Park at that time, and ran to meet him when he appeared in sight. But on the night of our hero's capture by Martin they waited for him in vain.

"Where can Rufie be?" thought Rose, as she heard six o'clock peal from a neighboring church-tower.

She thought he might have gone by without her seeing him, and with this idea, as it was already the hour for dinner, she went into the house. She ran upstairs two steps at a time, and opened the door of her own room.

"You should not have stayed out so late, Rose," said Miss Manning. "You will hardly have time to get ready for dinner."

"I was waiting for Rufie. Has he come?"

"No; he seems to be late to-night."

"I am afraid he's got run over," said Rose anxiously.

"Rufus is old enough to take care of himself. I've no doubt he's quite safe."

"Then what makes him so late?"

"He is probably detained by business. But there is the bell. We must go down to dinner."

"Can't we wait for Rufie?"

"No, my dear child; we cannot tell when he will be home."

"It don't seem a bit pleasant to eat dinner without Rufie," complained Rose.

"It isn't often he stays, Rose. He'll tell us all about it when he comes."

They went down and took their seats at the dinner-table.

"Where is your brother, Rose?" asked Mrs. Clifton.

"He hasn't got home," said Rose, rather disconsolately.

"I am sorry for that. He is a very agreeable young man. If I wasn't married," simpered Mrs. Clifton, "I should set my cap for him. But I mustn't say that, or Mr. Clifton will be jealous."

"Oh, don't mind me!" said Mr. Clifton, carelessly. "It won't spoil my appetite."

"I don't think there's anything that would spoil *your* appetite," said his wife, rather sharply, for she would have been flattered by her husband's jealousy.

"Just so," said Mr. Clifton, coolly. "May I trouble you for some chicken, Mrs. Clayton?"

"You're a great deal too old for Rufie, Mrs. Clifton," said Rose, with more plainness than politeness.

"I'm not quite so young as you are, Rose," said Mrs. Clifton, somewhat annoyed. "How old do you think I am?"

"Most fifty," answered Rose, honestly.

"Mercy sake!" exclaimed Mrs. Clifton, horrified, "what a child you are! Why don't you say a hundred, and done with it?"

"How old are you, Mrs. Clifton?" persisted Rose.

"Well, if you must know, I shall be twenty-five next November."

Mrs. Clifton was considerably nearer thirty-five; but, then, some ladies are very apt to be forgetful of their age.

The dinner-hour passed, and Rose and Miss Manning left the table. They went upstairs hoping that Rufus might be there before them; but the room was empty. An hour and a half passed, and it was already beyond eight, the hour at which Rose usually went to bed.

"Can't I sit up a little later to-night, Miss Manning?" pleaded Rose. "I want to see Rufie."

"No, Rose, I think not. You'll see him in the morning."

So Rose unwillingly undressed and went to bed.

By this time Miss Manning began to wonder a little why Rufus did not appear. It seemed to her rather strange that he should be detained by business till after eight o'clock, and she thought that an accident might possibly have happened to him. Still Rufus was a strong, manly boy, well able to take care of himself, and this was not probable.

When ten o'clock came, and he had not yet made his appearance, she went downstairs. The door of the hall bedroom, which Rufus occupied, was open and empty. This she saw on the way. In the hall below she met Mrs. Clayton.

"Rufus has not yet come in?" she said, interrogatively.

"No, I have not seen him. I saved some dinner for him, thinking he might have been detained."

"I can't think why he doesn't come home. I think he must be here soon. Do you know if he has a latch-key?"

"Yes, he got a new one of me the other day. Perhaps he has gone to some place of amusement."

"He would not go without letting us know beforehand. He would know we would feel anxious."

"Yes, he is more considerate than most young men of his age. I don't think you need feel anxious about him."

Miss Manning went upstairs disappointed. She began to feel perplexed and anxious. Suppose something should happen to Rufus, what would they do? Rose would refuse to be comforted. She was glad the little girl was asleep, otherwise she would be asking questions which she would be unable to answer. It was now her hour for retiring, but she resolved to sit up a little longer. More than an hour passed, and still Rufus did not come. It seemed unlikely that he would return that night, and Miss Manning saw that it was useless to sit up longer. It was possible, however, that he might have come in, and gone at once to his room, thinking it too late to disturb them. But, on going down to the next floor, she saw that his room was still unoccupied.

Rose woke up early in the morning; Miss Manning was already awake.

"Did Rufie come last night?" asked the little girl.

"He had not come when I went to bed," was the answer. "Perhaps he came in afterwards."

"May I dress and go down and see?"

"Yes, if you would like to."

Rose dressed quicker than usual, and went downstairs. She came up again directly, with a look of disappointment.

"Miss Manning, he is not here," she said. "His chamber door is open, and I saw that he had not slept in his bed."

"Very likely Mr. Turner sent him out of the city on business," said Miss Manning, with an indifference which she did not feel.

"I wish he'd come," said Rose. "I shall give him a good scolding, when he gets home, for staying away so long."

"Has not Mr. Rushton come?" asked Mrs. Clayton, at the breakfast-table.

"Not yet. I suppose he is detained by business."

Just after breakfast, Miss Manning, as usual, took the three little girls out in the Park to play. It was their custom to come in about nine o'clock to study. This morning, however, their governess went to Mrs. Colman and said, "I should like to take this morning, if you have no objection. I am feeling a little anxious about Rufus, who did not come home last night. I would like to go to the office where he is employed, and inquire whether he has been sent out of town on any errand."

"Certainly, Miss Manning. The little girls can go out and play in the Park while you are gone."

"Thank you."

"Where are you going, Miss Manning?" asked Rose, seeing that the governess was preparing to go out.

"I am going to Rufie's office to see why he stayed away."

"May I go with you?" asked Rose, eagerly.

"No, Rose, you had better stay at home. The streets are very crowded down town, and I shouldn't like to venture to cross Broadway with you. You can go and play in the Park."

"And shan't we have any lessons?"

"Not this morning."

"That will be nice," said Rose, who, like most girls of her age, enjoyed a holiday.

Miss Manning walked to Broadway, and took a stage. That she knew would carry her as far as Wall Street, only a few rods from Mr. Turner's office. She had seldom been in a stage, the stage fare being higher than in the cars, and even four cents made a difference to her. She would have enjoyed the brilliant scene which Broadway always presents, with its gay shop-windows and hurrying multitudes, if her mind had not been preoccupied. At length Trinity spire came in sight. When they reached the great church which forms so prominent a landmark in the lower part of Broadway, she got out, and turned into Wall Street.

It did not take her long to find Mr. Turner's number. She had never been there before, and had never met Mr. Turner, and naturally felt a little diffident about going into the office. It was on the second floor. She went up the stairway, and timidly entered. She looked about her, but Rufus was not to be seen. At first no one noticed her; but finally a clerk, with a pen behind his ear, came out from behind the line of desks.

"What can I do for you, ma'am?" he asked.

"Is Rufus Rushton here?" she inquired.

"No, he is not."

"Was he here yesterday?"

"He's out of the office just now, on some business of Mr. Turner's. That's Mr. Turner, if you would like to speak to him."

Miss Manning turned, and saw Mr. Turner just entering the office. He was a pleasant-looking man, and this gave her courage to address him.

"Mr. Turner," she said, "I came to ask about Rufus Rushton.

He did not come home last night, and I am feeling anxious about him."

"Indeed!" said the banker, "I am surprised to hear that. It leads me to think that he may have found a clue to the stolen box."

"The stolen box!" repeated Miss Manning, in surprise.

"Yes; did he not tell you of it?"

"No, sir."

Mr. Turner briefly related the particulars already known to the reader. "I think," he said, in conclusion, "Rufus must have tracked the man Martin, and—"

"Martin!" interrupted Miss Manning. "Was he the thief?"

"Yes, so Rufus tells me. Do you know him?"

"I have good reason to. He is a very bad man. I hope he has not got Rufus in his power."

"I don't think you need feel apprehensive. Rufus is a smart boy, and knows how to take care of himself. He'll come out right, I have no doubt."

"I am glad to hear you say so, Mr. Turner. I will bid you good-morning, with thanks for your kindness."

"If Rufus comes in this morning, I will let him go home at once, that your anxiety may be relieved."

With this assurance Miss Manning departed. She had learned something, but, in spite of the banker's assurance, she felt troubled. She knew Martin was a bad man, and she was afraid Rufus would come to harm.

CHAPTER XXII

MARTIN GROWS SUSPICIOUS

Our hero's interview with Humpy gave him new courage. When he had felt surrounded by enemies the chances seemed against him. Now he had a friend in the house, who was interested in securing his escape. Not only this, but there was a fair chance of recovering the box for which he was seeking. On the whole, therefore, Rufus was in very good spirits.

About nine o'clock he heard a step on the stairs, which he recognized as that of his step-father. He had good reason to remember that step. Many a time while his mother was alive, and afterwards while they were living in Leonard Street, he had listened to it coming up the rickety staircase, and dreaded the entrance of the man whose presence was never welcome.

After some fumbling at the lock the door opened, and Martin entered. It was dark, and he could not at first see Rufus.

"Where are you, you young villain?" he inquired, with a hiccough.

Rufus did not see fit to answer when thus addressed.

"Where are you, I say?" repeated Martin.

"Here I am," answered Rufus.

"Why didn't you speak before? Didn't you hear me?" demanded his step-father, angrily.

"Yes, Mr. Martin, I heard you," said Rufus, composedly.

"Then why didn't you answer?"

"Because you called me a young villain."

"Well, you are one."

Rufus did not answer.

Martin locked the door and put the key in his pocket. He next struck a match, and lit the gas. Then seating himself in a rocking-chair, still with his hat on, he looked at Rufus with some curiosity, mingled with triumph.

"I hope you like your accommodations," he said.

"Pretty well."

"We don't charge you nothing for board, you see, and you haven't any work to do. That's what I call living like a gentleman."

"I believe you tried the same kind of life at Blackwell's Island," said Rufus.

"Look here," said Martin, roughly, "you'd better not insult me. I didn't come here to be insulted."

"What did you come for, then?" asked Rufus.

"I thought you'd like to know how Rose was," answered Martin.

"I don't believe you have seen her."

"Well, you needn't believe it. Perhaps I didn't meet her on the street, and follow her home. She begged me to tell her where you was; but I couldn't do it."

Rufus felt a temporary uneasiness when he heard this statement; but there was something in Martin's manner which convinced him that he had not been telling the truth. He decided to change the subject.

"Mr. Martin," he said, "have you made up your mind to give up that tin box?"

"No I haven't. I can't spare it."

"If you will give it up, I will see that you are not punished for taking it."

"I aint a-goin' to be punished for taking it."

"You certainly will be if you are caught."

"What do you know about it?"

"There was a man convicted of the same thing three months ago, and he got five years for it."

"I don't believe it," said Martin, uneasily.

"You needn't if you don't want to."

"I haven't got the box now, so I couldn't give it back. Smith's got it."

"Is that the man I saw this morning?"

"Yes."

"Then you'd better ask him to give it back to you."

"He wouldn't do it if I asked him."

"Then I'm sorry for you."

Martin was not very brave, and in spite of his assertions he felt uneasy at what Rufus was saying. Besides, he felt rather afraid of our hero. He knew that Rufus was a resolute, determined boy, and that he could not keep him confined forever. Some time he would get out, and Martin feared that he would set the officers on his track. The remark of Smith that he would make a good boy for their business occurred to him, and he determined to try him on a new tack. If he could get him compromised by a connection with their business, it would be for his interest also to keep clear of the police.

"Rufus," said Martin, edging his chair towards our hero, "I'm your friend."

Rufus was rather astonished at this sudden declaration.

"I'm glad to hear it," he said; "but I don't think you've treated me in a very friendly manner."

"About the tin box?"

"Yes, partly that. If you're my friend, you will return it, and not keep me locked up here."

"Never mind, Rufus, I've got a business proposal to make to you. You're a smart boy."

"I am glad you think so."

"And I can give you a chance to make a good living."

"I am making a good living now, or I was before you interfered with me."

"How much did you earn a week?"

"Why do you want to know?"

"Was it over ten dollars a week?"

"About that."

"I know a business that will pay you fifteen dollars a week."

"What is it?"

"It is the one I'm in. I earn a hundred dollars a month."

"If you are earning as much as that, I shouldn't think you'd need to steal tin boxes."

"There wasn't much in it. Only a hundred dollars in money."

"You are not telling me the truth. There were four hundred dollars in it."

"What was that you said?" asked Martin, pricking up his ears.

"There were four hundred dollars in it."

"How do you know?"

"Mr. Turner told me so."

"Smith told me there were only a hundred. He opened it, and gave me half."

"Then he gave you fifty, and kept three hundred and fifty himself."

"If I thought that, I'd smash his head!" said Martin, angrily. "Make me run all the risk, and then cheat me out of my hard earnin's. Do you call that fair?"

"I think he's been cheating you," said Rufus, not sorry to see Martin's anger with his confederate.

"It's a mean trick," said Martin, indignantly. "I'd ought to have got two hundred. It was worth it."

"I wouldn't do what you did for a good deal more than two hundred dollars. You haven't told me what that business was that I could earn fifteen dollars a week at."

"No," said Martin, "I've changed my mind about it. If Smith's goin' to serve me such a mean trick, I won't work for him no longer. I'll speak to him about it to-morrow."

Martin relapsed into silence. Rufus had given him something to think about, which disturbed him considerably. Though he had been disappointed in the contents of the box, he had not for a moment doubted the good faith of his confederate, and he was proportionately incensed now that the latter had appropriated seven dollars to his one. Considering that he had done all the work, and incurred all the danger, it did seem rather hard.

There was one bed in the room, rather a narrow one.

"I'm goin' to bed," said Martin, at length. "I guess the bed'll be big enough for us both."

"Thank you," said Rufus, who did not fancy the idea of sleeping with his step-father. "If you'll give me one of the pillows, I'll sleep on the floor."

"Just as you say, but you'll find it rather hard sleepin'."

"I shan't mind."

This was the arrangement they adopted. Martin took off his coat and vest, and threw himself on the bed. He was soon asleep, as his heavy breathing clearly indicated. Rufus, stretched on the floor, lay awake longer. It occurred to him that he might easily take the key of the door from the pocket of Martin's vest, which lay on the chair at his bedside, and so let himself out of the room. But even then it would be uncertain whether he could get out of the house, and he would have to leave the tin box behind him. This he hoped to get hold of through Humpy's assistance. On the whole, therefore, it seemed best to wait a little longer.

CHAPTER XXIII

ESCAPE

Humpy made up his mind to accept our hero's offer. Fifty dollars was to him a small fortune, and he saw no reason why he should not earn it. The brutal treatment he had received from Smith removed all the objections he had at first felt.

Now, how was he going to fulfil his part of the compact?

To release Rufus would be comparatively easy. He happened to know that the key of his own room in the attic would also fit the door of the chamber in which our hero was confined. The difficulty was to get possession of the tin box. He did not even know where it was concealed, and must trust to his own sagacity to find out.

To this end he watched his employer carefully whenever he got a chance to do so without being observed, hoping he might take the box out from its place of concealment. Finally Smith noticed the boy's glances, and said, roughly, "What are you looking at, boy? Do you think you shall know me the next time you see me?"

Humpy did not reply, but this made him more careful.

In the morning he took up our hero's breakfast, meeting Martin on his way downstairs.

"Well," said Rufus, eagerly, as he entered the room, "have you found out anything about the box?"

"Not yet," said Humpy. "I'm tryin' to find where he's hid it. I can let you out any time."

"How?"

"I've got a key that fits this lock."

"That's well, but I'd rather wait till I can carry the box with me."

"I'll do what I can," said Humpy. "I'm goin' to watch him sharp. I'd better go down now, or maybe he'll be suspectin' something."

Humpy went downstairs, leaving Rufus to eat his breakfast. On his way down his attention was drawn by angry voices, proceeding from the room in which he had left Smith. He comprehended at once that Smith and Martin were having a dispute about something. He stood still and listened attentively, and caught the following conversation:—

"The boy tells me," said Martin, doggedly, "that there was four hundred dollars in the box. You only gave me fifty."

"Then the boy lies!" said Smith, irritated.

"I don't believe he does," said Martin. "I don't like him myself, but he aint in the habit of telling lies."

"Perhaps you believe him sooner than you do me."

"I don't see where the three hundred dollars went," persisted Martin. "Considerin' that I did all the work, fifty dollars was very small for me."

"You got half what there was. If there'd been more, you'd have got more."

"Why didn't you wait and open the box when I was there?"

"Look here," said Smith, menacingly, "if you think I cheated you, you might as well say so right out. I don't like beating around the bush."

"The boy says there was four hundred dollars. Turner told him so."

"Then Turner lies!" exclaimed Smith, who was the more angry, because the charge was a true one. "The box is just as it was when I opened it. I'll bring it out and show you just where I found the money."

When Humpy heard this, his eyes sparkled with excitement and anticipation. Now, if ever, he would find out the whereabouts of the tin box. Luckily for him the door was just ajar, and by standing on the upper part of the staircase he could manage to see into the room.

He saw Smith go to a desk at the centre of one side of the room, and open a drawer in it. From this he drew out the box, and, opening it, displayed the contents to Martin.

"There," said he, "that's where I found the money. There was a roll of ten ten-dollar bills. I divided them into two equal parts, and gave you your share. I was disappointed myself, for I expected more. I didn't think you'd suspect me of cheating you. But I don't want any fuss. I'll give you ten dollars off my share, and then you can't complain."

So saying, he took out a ten from his pocket-book, and handed it to Martin.

"Are you satisfied now?" he asked.

"I suppose I shall have to be," said Martin, rather sullenly, for he was by no means sure of the veracity of his confederate.

"It's all I can do for you at any rate," said Smith. "And now suppose we take breakfast. I shall want you to go to Newark to-day."

He replaced the box in the drawer, and, locking it, put the key in his pocket.

By this time Humpy thought it would do to reappear.

"Where've you been all the time?" asked Smith, roughly.

"The boy upstairs was talkin' to me."

"What did he say?"

"He asked what was your business."

"What did you tell him?"

"I told him I didn't rightly know; but I thought you was a manufacturer."

"Right, Humpy; you're a smart boy," laughed Smith. "You know a thing or two."

The boy showed his teeth, and appeared pleased with the compliment.

"What else did he ask?"

"He asked, would I let him out?"

"Did he, the young rascal? And what did you tell him?"

"Not for Joe!"

"Good for you! There's a quarter;" and Smith offered the boy twenty-five cents.

"If he'd done that yesterday instead of hittin' me," thought Humpy, "I wouldn't have gone ag'inst him."

But the money came too late. Humpy had a brooding sense of wrong, not easily removed, and he had made up his mind to betray his employer.

The breakfast proceeded, Humpy waiting upon the table. When the meal was over, Smith gave Martin some instructions, and the latter set out for Newark, which was to be the scene of his operations during the day. About half an hour later Smith said, "Humpy, I've got to go down town; I may be gone all the forenoon. Stay in the house while I am gone, and look out, above all, that that boy upstairs don't escape."

"Yes, sir," said Humpy.

When Smith left, the coast was clear. There were none in the house except Rufus and the boy who was expected to stand guard over him. The giant had gone to Philadelphia on some business, precisely what Humpy did not understand, and there was nothing to prevent his carrying out his plans.

He had two or three old keys in his pocket, and with these he eagerly tried the lock of the drawer. But none exactly fitted. One was too large, the other two were too small.

Humpy decided what to do. He left the house, and went to a neighboring locksmith.

"I want to get a key," he said.

"What size?"

"A little smaller than this."

"I must know the exact size, or I can't suit you. What is it the key of?"

"A drawer."

"I can go with you to the house."

"That won't do," said Humpy. "I've lost the key, and I don't want the boss to know it. He'd find out if you went to the house."

"Then I'll tell you what you can do. Take an impression of the lock in wax. I'll give you some wax, and show you how. Then I'll make a key for you."

"Can you do it right off? I'm in a great hurry."

"Yes, my son, I'll attend to it right away."

He brought a piece of wax, and showed Humpy how to take an impression of a lock.

"There," said he, laughing, "that's the first lesson in burglary."

Humpy lost no time in hurrying back and following the locksmith's instructions. He then returned to the shop.

"How soon can I have the key?"

"In an hour. I'm pretty sure I've got a key that will fit this impression with a little filing down. Come back in an hour, and you shall have it."

Humpy went back, and seeing that there were some traces of wax on the lock, he carefully washed them off with soap. A little before the hour was up, he reported himself at the locksmith's.

"Your key is all ready for you," said the smith. "I guess it will answer."

"How much is it?"

"Twenty-five cents."

Humpy paid the money, and hurried to the house, anxious to make his experiment.

The locksmith's assurance was verified. The key did answer. The drawer opened, and the errand-boy's eyes sparkled with pleasure as they rested on the box. He snatched it, hastily relocked the drawer, and went up the stairs two at a time. He had the key of his attic room in his pocket. With this he opened the door of the chamber, and, entering triumphantly, displayed to Rufus the tin box.

"I've got it!" he ejaculated.

Rufus sprang to his feet, and hurried up to him.

"You're a trump!" he said. "How did you get hold of it?"

"I haven't time to tell you now. We must be goin', or Mr. Smith may come back and stop us."

"All right!" said Rufus; "I'm ready."

The two boys ran downstairs, and, opening the front door, made their egress into the street, Rufus with the tin box under his arm.

"Where will we go?" asked Humpy.

"Are you going with me?"

"Yes, I want that money."

"You shall have it. You have fairly earned it, and I'll see that you get it, if I have to pay it out of my own pocket."

"I shan't go back," said Humpy.

"Why not?"

"He'll know I let you out. He'll murder me if I go back."

"I'll be your friend. I'll get you something to do," said Rufus.

"Will you?" said the hunchback, brightening up.

"Yes. I won't forget the service you have done me."

Rufus had hardly got out these words when Humpy clutched him violently by the arm, and pulled him into a passageway, the door of which was open to the street.

"What's that for?" demanded Rufus, inclined to be angry.

Humpy put his finger to his lip, and pointed to the street. On the opposite sidewalk Rufus saw Smith sauntering easily along with a cigar in his mouth.

CHAPTER XXIV

HOW RUFUS GOT BACK

It happened that Smith espied the man whom he wished to meet, from the car-window, just as it turned into Canal Street. He got out, therefore, and, adjourning to a whiskey saloon, the two discussed a matter of business in which they were jointly interested, and then separated. Thus Smith was enabled to return home sooner than he had anticipated. He little suspected that his prisoner had escaped, as he walked complacently by on the opposite sidewalk.

"It's lucky I saw him," said Humpy. "He might have nabbed us."

"He wouldn't have nabbed me," said Rufus, resolutely. "He'd have found it hard work to get me back."

"He's stronger than you," said Humpy, doubtfully.

"I'd have called a copp, then," said Rufus, using his old word for policeman.

"He'll kill me if he ever gets hold of me," said Humpy, shuddering. "He horsewhipped me yesterday."

"Then he's a brute," said Rufus, who could not help feeling a degree of sympathy for the deformed boy, who had done him such good service.

"He never did it before," said Humpy. "That's what made me turn against him."

"And you won't go back to him?"

"*Never!*" said Humpy, decidedly. "He'll know I let you out."

"What's your name?" asked Rufus, remembering that he had never heard the name of his guide.

"They call me Humpy," said the deformed boy, flushing a little. He had got hardened to the name, he thought; but now that Rufus asked him, he answered with a feeling of shame and reluctance.

"Haven't you another name? I don't like to call you that."

"My name is William Norton, but I've most forgot it, it's so long since anybody ever called me so."

"Then I'll call you so. I like it better than the other. Have you made up your mind what to do, now you've left your old place?"

"Yes, I'm going out West,—to Chicago maybe."

"Why do you leave New York?"

"I want to get away from *him*," said William, indicating his old employer by a backward jerk of his finger. "If I stay here, he'll get hold of me."

"Perhaps you are right; but you needn't go so far as Chicago. Philadelphia would do."

"He goes there sometimes."

"What will you do in Chicago?"

"I'll get along. There's a good many things I can do,—black boots, sell papers, smash baggage, and so on. Besides, I'll have some money."

"The fifty dollars I am to give you?"

"I've got more besides," said Humpy, lowering his voice. Looking around cautiously, lest he might be observed, he drew out the calico bag which contained his savings, and showed to Rufus.

"There's twenty dollars in that," he said, jingling the coins with an air of satisfaction. "That'll make seventy when you've paid me."

"I'm glad you've got so much, William. Where did you get it all?"

"I saved it up. He paid me fifty cents a week, and gave me an extra quarter or so sometimes when he felt good-natured. I saved it all up, and here it is."

"When did you begin saving?"

"Six months ago. I used to spend all my money for oysters and cigars, but somebody told me smokin' would stop me from growin', and I gave it up."

"You did right. I used to smoke sometimes; but I stopped. It don't do a boy any good."

"Are you rich?" asked Humpy.

"No. What makes you ask?"

"You wear nice clo'es. Besides, you are goin' to pay me fifty dollars."

"I'm worth five hundred dollars," said Rufus, with satisfaction.

"That's a good deal," said Humpy, enviously. "I'd feel rich if I had so much."

"You'll be worth a good deal more some time, I hope."

"I hope so, but it'll be a good while."

While this conversation had been going on, the boys had been walking leisurely. But Rufus, who was anxious to restore the tin box as soon as possible, now proposed to ride.

"We'll jump aboard the next car, William," he said. "I'll pay the fare."

"Where are you goin'?"

"To Mr. Turner's office, to return the box."

"He won't think I had anything to do with stealin' it, will he?"

"No; I'll take care he doesn't."

They jumped on board the next car, and before long reached the termination of the car route, at the junction of Vesey Street and Broadway.

"Where's the place you're goin' to?" asked Humpy.

"In Wall Street. We'll be there in ten minutes."

The boys proceeded down Broadway, and in rather less than ten minutes, Rufus, followed by Humpy, entered his employer's office.

His arrival created a sensation.

"I am glad to see you back, Rufus," said Mr. Turner, coming forward, and shaking his hand cordially.

The clerks left their desks, and greeted him in a friendly manner.

"I've brought back the tin box, Mr. Turner," said Rufus. "I told you I'd get it back, and I have," he added, with pardonable pride.

"How did you recover it? Tell me all about it."

"This boy helped me," said Rufus, directing attention to Humpy, who had kept himself in the background. "But for him I should still be a prisoner, closely confined and guarded."

"He shall be rewarded," said the banker. "What is his name?"

"William Morton."

Mr. Turner took the boy's hand kindly, dirty though it was, and said, "I will bear you in mind, my lad," in a tone which made Humpy, who before felt awkward and uncertain of a welcome, quite at his ease.

"Now for your story, Rufus," said the banker. "I am curious to hear your adventures. So you were a prisoner?"

"Yes, sir," answered Rufus, and forthwith commenced a clear and straightforward account of his experiences, which need not be repeated. He wound up by saying that he had promised Humpy fifty dollars in return for his assistance.

"Your promise shall be kept," said Mr. Turner. "I will pay you the money now, if you wish," he added, turning to Humpy. "I would advise you to put most of it in a savings-bank, as you are liable to be robbed, or to lose it."

"I'll put it in as soon as I get to Chicago," said Humpy.

"Are you going there?"

Rufus explained why the boy wished to leave New York.

"Do you want to start at once?"

"I'd like to."

"Then, Rufus, I think you had better go with him, and buy his ticket. You may also buy him a suit of clothes at my expense."

"Thank you, sir," said Humpy, gratefully.

"If you can spare me, Mr. Turner," said Rufus, "I would like to go home first, and let them know that I am safe."

"Certainly. That reminds me that a lady—was it your aunt?—was in the office an hour ago, asking for you."

"It was Miss Manning."

"I promised to let you go home when you appeared, and I think you had better do so at once to relieve the anxiety of your friends."

"Thank you, sir;" and Rufus was about to leave the office, when a thought occurred to him, and he turned back.

"I didn't think to tell you that the money had been taken out," he said.

"So I supposed. I will open the box."

The box being opened, it was discovered also that the government bonds were missing.

"That's too much to lose," said the banker. "What is the number of the house in which you were confined?"

Rufus was able to give it, having judged that it would be wanted.

"I shall give information to the police, and see what can be done towards recovering the bonds."

"Shall I go to the police-office for you, Mr. Turner?"

"No, you can go home at once. Then accompany this boy to a clothing-store, and afterwards to the Erie Railroad Station, where you may buy him a through ticket to Chicago. Here is the necessary money;" and Mr. Turner placed a roll of bills in the hands of our hero.

"Am I to buy the railroad ticket, also, out of this?"

"Yes. William shall have his fifty dollars clear to start on when he gets there."

Miss Manning had nearly got through with the morning lessons, when a quick step was heard ascending the stairs two or three at a time. Rose let drop the arithmetic, from which she had been reciting, and exclaimed, in glad excitement, "That's Rufie, I know it is!"

The door opened, and she was proved to be correct.

"Where've you been, Rufie?" exclaimed his sister, throwing her arms around his neck.

"Mr. Martin carried me off, Rosy."

"I knew he would; but you said you was too big."

"He was smarter than I thought for. Sit down, Rosy, and I'll tell you all about it. Were you anxious about me, Miss Manning?"

"Yes, Rufus. I don't mind saying now that I was, though I would not confess it to Rose, who fretted enough for you without."

So the story had to be told again, and was listened to, I need not say, with breathless interest.

"You won't let him catch you again, will you, Rufie?" said Rose, anxiously, when it was finished.

"Not if I know myself, Rosy," answered Rufus. "That can't be done twice. But I've got to be going. I've got ever so much to do. I'll be back to dinner at six."

He hastened downstairs, and rejoined Humpy, who had been waiting for him in the street.

CHAPTER XXV

UNPLEASANT DISCOVERIES

Smith did not go home immediately. He intended to do so, but happened to think of an errand, and this delayed him for an hour or two.

When he entered the house, he looked around for his errand-boy, but looked in vain.

"Humpy!" he called out in a voice which could be heard all over the house.

There was no answer. Smith, who was not remarkable for patience, began to grow angry.

"Very likely the young rascal is in his room," he said to himself. "I'll stir him up."

He took the whip and ascended the stairs two or three at a time. Arrived in the attic, he peered into Humpy's room, but, to his disappointment, saw nobody.

"The little villain got tired of waiting, and went out, thinking I couldn't find him out," he muttered. "He shall have a taste of the whip when he comes back."

He went downstairs more slowly than he ascended. He was considerably irritated, and in a state that required an object to vent his anger upon. Under these circumstances his prisoner naturally occurred to him. He had the proper key in his pocket, and, stopping on the second floor, he opened the door of the chamber in which our hero had been confined. His anger may be imagined when he found it untenanted. It was not very dignified, but Smith began to stamp in his vexation, and lash with his whip an unoffending chair in which Rufus ought to have been seated.

"I wish it was that young villain!" muttered Smith, scowling at the chair, and lashing it harder. "I'd teach him to run away! I'd make him howl!"

Smith was considerably discomposed. Things were going decidedly against him. Besides, the escape of Rufus might entail serious consequences, if he should give information to the police about the place of his captivity. A visit from these officials was an honor which Smith felt disposed respectfully, but firmly, to decline. Unfortunately, however, policemen are not sensitive, and are very apt to intrude where they are not wanted. A visit to Smith's abode might lead to unpleasant discoveries, as he very well knew, and he could not easily decide what course it would be best for him to pursue. He inferred at once that Humpy had been bought over, and had released the prisoner, otherwise he would, undoubtedly, have detected or frustrated our hero's attempt to escape. This did not inspire very amiable feelings towards Humpy, whom it would have yielded him great satisfaction to get into his power. But Humpy had disappeared, and that satisfaction was not to be had.

Mingled with Smith's anger was a feeling of surprise. Humpy had been a good while in his employ, and he had reposed entire confidence in his fidelity. He might have continued to do so but for the brutal assault upon the boy recorded in a previous chapter. He did not think of this, however, or guess the effect it had produced on the mind of the deformed errand-boy.

"I think I had better get out of the city a week or two till this blows over," thought Smith. "I guess I'll take the afternoon train for Philadelphia."

This was a wise resolution; but Smith made one mistake. He ought to have put it into effect at once. At that very moment information was lodged at the office of police, which threatened serious consequences to him; but of this he was ignorant. He had no idea that Rufus would act so promptly.

In spite of his anger Smith was hungry. His morning walk had given him an excellent appetite, and he began to think about dinner. As, on account of the unlawful occupation in which he was engaged, he did not think it prudent to employ a cook, who might gossip about his affairs, he generally devolved the task of preparing the dinner upon Humpy, whom he had taught to cook eggs, broil beef-steak, make coffee, fry potatoes, and perform other simple culinary duties. Now that Humpy was gone, he was obliged to do this work himself.

He looked into the pantry, and found half-a-dozen eggs, and a slice of steak. These he proceeded to cook. He had nearly finished his unaccustomed task when the door opened, and Martin returned, with his nose a little redder than usual, and his general appearance somewhat disordered by haste.

"What brings you here so soon?" asked Smith, in surprise. "What's the matter?"

"I came near gettin' nabbed; that's what's the matter," said Martin.

"How did that happen?"

"I went into a cigar-store near the ferry in Jersey City," said Martin, "and asked for a couple of cigars,—twenty-cent ones. I took 'em, and handed in one of your ten-dollar bills. The chap looked hard at it, and then at me, and said he'd have to go out and get it changed. I looked across the street, and saw him goin' to the police-office. I thought I'd better leave, and made for the ferry. The boat was just goin'. When we'd got a little ways out, I saw the cigar man standin' on the drop with a copp at his elbow."

"You'd better not go to Jersey City again," said Smith.

"I don't mean to," said Martin. "Have you got enough dinner for me? I'm as hungry as a dog."

"Yes, there's dinner enough for two, and that's all there is to eat it."

Something significant in his employer's tone struck Martin.

"There's the boy upstairs," he said.

"There isn't any boy upstairs."

"You haven't let him go?" queried Martin, staring open-mouthed at the speaker.

"No, he got away while I was out this morning,—the more fool I for leaving him."

"But there was Humpy. How did the boy get away without his seeing him?"

"Humpy's gone too."

"You don't say!" ejaculated Martin.

"Yes, I do."

"What you goin' to do about it?" inquired Martin, hopelessly.

"I'll half kill either of the little rascals when I get hold of them," said Smith, spitefully.

"I'd give something out of my own pocket to get that undootiful son of mine back," chimed in Martin.

"I'll say this for him," said Smith, "he's a good sight smarter than his father."

"I always was unlucky," grumbled Martin. "I aint been treated right."

"If you had been you'd be at Sing Sing," returned Smith, amiably.

"Smith," said Martin, with drunken dignity, for he was somewhat under the influence of a liberal morning dram, "you'd ought to respect the feelin's of a gentleman."

"Where's the gentleman? I don't see him," responded Smith, in a sarcastic tone. "If you aint too much of a gentleman to do your share of the work, just draw out the table and put the cloth on."

This Martin, who was hungry, did with equal alacrity and awkwardness, showing the latter by over-turning a pile of plates, which fell with a fatal crash upon the floor.

"Just like your awkwardness, you drunken brute!" exclaimed Smith, provoked.

Martin did not reply, but looked ruefully at the heap of broken crockery, which he attributed, like his other misfortunes, to the ill-treatment of the world, and meekly got upon his knees and gathered up the pieces.

At length dinner was ready. Martin, in spite of an ungrateful world, ate with an appetite truly surprising, so that his companion felt called upon to remonstrate.

"I hope you'll leave a little for me. It's just possible that I might like to eat a little something myself."

"I didn't eat much breakfast," said Martin, apologetically.

"You'd better lunch outside next time," said his employer. "It will give you a good chance to change money."

"I've tried it at several places," said Martin; "I could do it better if you'd give me some smaller bills. They don't like to change fives and tens."

After dinner was despatched, and the table pushed back, Smith unfolded his plans to Martin. He suggested that it might be a little unsafe to remain at their present quarters for a week or fortnight to come, and counselled Martin to go to Boston, while he would go to Philadelphia.

"That's the way we'll dodge them," he concluded.

"Just as you say," said Martin. "When do you want me back?"

"I will write you from Philadelphia. You can call at the post-office for a letter in a few days."

"When had I better sell the bond?"

"That reminds me," said Smith. "I will take the box with me."

He went and unlocked the drawer in which the box had been secreted. To his dismay he discovered that it was gone.

"Have you taken the tin box?" he demanded, turning upon Martin with sudden suspicion.

"Isn't it there?" gasped Martin.

"No, it isn't," said Smith, sternly. "Do you know anything about it?"

"I wish I may be killed if I do!" asserted Martin.

"Then what can have become of it?"

"It's my undootiful boy that took it,—I'm sure it is," exclaimed Martin, with sudden conviction.

"He had no key."

"Humpy got him one, then."

Just then Smith espied on the floor some scraps of wax. They told the story.

"You're right," he said, with an oath. "We've been taken in worse than I thought. The best thing we can do is to get away as soon as possible."

They made a few hurried preparations, and left the house in company. But they were too late. A couple of officers, who were waiting outside, stepped up to them, as they set foot on the sidewalk, and said, quietly, "You must come with us."

"What for?" demanded Smith, inclined to show fight.

"You'd better come quietly. You are charged with stealing a box containing valuables."

"That's the man that did it," said Smith, pointing to Martin. "He's the one you want."

"He put me up to it, and shared the money," retorted Martin.

"You're both wanted," said the officer. "You'll have a chance to tell your story hereafter."

As this winds up the connection of these two worthies with our story, it may be added here that they were found guilty, not only of the robbery, but of manufacturing and disseminating counterfeit money, and were sentenced to Sing Sing for a term of years. The bonds were found upon them, and restored to Mr. Vanderpool.

Thus the world persists in its ill-treatment of our friend, James Martin. Still I cannot help thinking that, if he had been a sober and industrious man, he would have had much less occasion to complain.

CHAPTER XXVI

CONCLUSION

In the course of an hour Humpy was provided with a new suit, which considerably improved his appearance. Rufus accompanied him to the Erie Railway Station, where he purchased for him a through ticket to Chicago, and saw him enter the cars.

"Good-by, William, and good luck!" said Rufus.

"Good-by," said Humpy. "You're a trump. You're the first friend I ever had."

"I hope I shan't be the last," said Rufus. "Shall I give your love to Smith, if I see him?"

"Never mind about it."

Rufus was compelled to leave the station before the cars started, in order to hurry back to the office. Arrived there a new errand awaited him.

"Rufus," said Mr. Turner, "do you remember where Mr. Vanderpool lives?"

"The owner of the tin box? Yes, sir."

"You may go up at once, and let him know that his property is recovered."

This task Rufus undertook with alacrity. He had been pleased with what he saw of Mr. Vanderpool on his first visit, and was glad to be able to tell him that the box, for whose loss he felt partly to blame, was recovered.

He was soon ringing the bell of the house in Twenty-Seventh Street.

Mr. Vanderpool was at home, the servant told him, and he was ushered immediately into his presence.

The old gentleman, who had been writing, laid aside his pen, and, looking up, recognized Rufus.

"You're the boy that came to tell me about my property being stolen, are you not?" he asked.

"Yes, sir; but it's found."

"Bless my soul, you don't say so! Did the thief give it up?"

"No," said Rufus. "I took it from him."

"Is it possible? Why, you're only a boy," said Mr. Vanderpool, regarding him with interest.

"Boys can do something as well as men," said Rufus, with pardonable pride.

"Tell me all about it."

Rufus told his story as briefly as possible. When he described how he had been entrapped and imprisoned, Mr. Vanderpool said, "Bless my soul!" several times.

"You're a brave boy!" he said, when the story was finished.

"Thank you, sir," said Rufus, modestly.

"Were you not afraid when you were locked up by those bad men?"

"Not at all, sir."

"I should have been. I don't think I am very brave. You've behaved very well indeed, Master —— I don't remember your name."

"Rufus Rushton."

"Master Rushton, I must make you a present."

"I have only done my duty, Mr. Vanderpool. I don't want any present for that."

"We'll talk about that afterwards. By the way, have you thought anything more about the question whether the planets are inhabited?"

"I can't say I have, sir. I've had so much else to think about."

"Very true, very true. I've written a few pages more, which I will read to you if you have time."

"I should like very much to hear them, sir; but I am afraid I must hurry back to the office."

"Ah, I am sorry for that," said the old gentleman, in a tone of disappointment, but he brightened up immediately.

"I'll tell you what, my young friend," he said; "you shall come and dine with me next Saturday at six, and then we will have the evening to ourselves. What do you say?"

"I shall be very happy to come, sir," said Rufus, not quite sure whether he would be happy or not.

When Saturday came he presented himself, and was very cordially received by the old gentleman. The dinner was a capital one, and served in excellent style. Mr. Vanderpool paid Rufus as much attention as if he were a guest of distinction,—read him his essay on the planets, and showed him some choice engravings. The evening passed very agreeably, and Rufus was urged to come again. He did so, and so won the favor of the old gentleman that at the end of two months he was invited to come and make his home permanently in the house in Twenty-Seventh Street.

"Thank you, Mr. Vanderpool," said our hero. "You are very kind; but I shouldn't like to leave Miss Manning and my little sister."

"Have you a little sister? Tell me about her."

"Her name is Rose, and she is a dear little girl," said Rufus, warmly.

"How old is she?"

"Eight years old."

"I am glad she is not a young lady. You can bring her too. I've got plenty of room. Who is Miss Manning?"

"She is a friend of mine, and teaches my sister."

"Why can't she come and look after my servants? I have no house-keeper."

"I will mention it to her," said Rufus.

Rufus did mention it to Miss Manning, who by appointment called upon the old gentleman. Mr. Vanderpool repeated the invitation, and offered her ten dollars per week for her services. Such an offer was not to be rejected. Miss Manning resigned her situation as governess to Mrs. Colman's children, greatly to that lady's disappointment, and removed with Rose to the house of Mr. Vanderpool. Elegant chambers were assigned to all three, and they found themselves living in fashionable style. As neither had any board to pay, Rufus felt justified in dressing both Rose and himself in a manner more befitting the style in which they now lived, while Miss Manning also, finding that she was expected to preside at the table, felt called upon to follow their example. It was such a change for all three that it seemed like a dream sometimes when they recalled the miserable attic in Leonard Street, and the humble lodging near the North River.

Rose was sent to school, and had a music-teacher at home. Miss Manning also, having considerable time at her disposal, took lessons in music and French, and soon acquired very respectable proficiency in both. The old gentleman, so long accustomed to solitude, seemed to renew his youth in the cheerful society he had gathered around him, and came to look upon Rufus and Rose as his own children. He was continually loading them with gifts, and his kindness won their gratitude and affection. He tried to induce Rufus to give up his situation with the banker; but our hero was of an independent turn, and had too active a temperament to be content with doing nothing. On the succeeding Christmas he received from Mr. Vanderpool a very costly gold watch, which I need not say was very acceptable.

About six months after her entrance into the house, Miss Manning was profoundly astonished by receiving from the old gentleman an offer of marriage.

"I don't ask for romantic love, my dear Miss Manning," said Mr. Vanderpool, "but I hope you will not find it hard to like me a little, and I'll try to make you happy. I don't want to hurry you. Take a week to think of it."

Miss Manning did take a week to think of it. She was not in love with Mr. Vanderpool,—that was hardly to be expected, as he was thirty years older than she,—but she did respect and esteem him, and she knew that he would be kind to her. So she said yes, after consulting with Rufus, and one morning, without any fuss or ostentation, she was quietly married, and transformed from plain Miss Manning into the rich Mrs. Vanderpool. I may say here that neither she nor her husband has seen cause to repent the match, so unexpectedly brought about, but live in harmony and mutual friendship, as I hope they may continue to do to the end of their days.

When Rufus reached the age of twenty-one, he was agreeably surprised by an offer from Mr. Turner to take him into partnership.

"But, Mr. Turner," he said, "I have very little capital,—far too little for a partner in such a large business."

"You have fifty thousand dollars. That will answer very well."

"I don't understand you, sir," said Rufus, suspecting that Mr. Turner was crazy, or was dreaming.

"You remember the tin box which you recovered five years ago?"

"Yes, sir."

"Mr. Vanderpool has made it over with its contents to you as a free gift. Its value, as you remember, is fifty thousand dollars, or rather more now, some of the stocks having risen in value."

Rufus was quite affected by this munificent gift, and no longer objected to the plan proposed. Shortly after, the style of the firm was changed, and now, as you pass through Wall Street, if you will closely examine the signs on either side of the street, your eyes may light on this one:—

Turner and Rushton, Bankers.

You will have no trouble in conjecturing that the junior partner in this firm is the same who was first known to you as Rough and Ready. If you think that our young friend, the newsboy, has had rare luck, I hope you will also admit that, by his honesty, industry, and generous protection of his little sister, he has deserved the prosperity he has attained.

George Black has long since bought out his partner's interest in the periodical store, and now carries on quite a flourishing trade in his own name. Smith and Martin are still in prison, their term of confinement not yet having expired. What adventures yet remain in store for James Martin I am unable to say, but I doubt if he will ever turn over a new leaf. His habits of indolence and intemperance are too confirmed to give much hope of amendment.

The fortunes of Rough and Ready, so far as this record is concerned, are now ended, and with them is completed the sixth and concluding volume of the Ragged Dick Series. But the flattering interest which his young friends have taken in these pictures of street life leads the author to announce the initial volume of a new series of stories of similar character, which will soon be published under the name of

Tattered Tom:

or,

The Adventures of a Street Arab.

CPSIA information can be obtained
at www.ICGtesting.com
Printed in the USA
LVOW13s1023020617

536727LV00018B/307/P